CUSTOMER SERVICE EXCELLENCE   **Libraries & Archives**

00884\DTP\RN\07.07   LIB 7

A PLACE OF HER OWN

A PLACE OF HER OWN

Miranda Barnes

CHIVERS

British Library Cataloguing in Publication Data available

This Large Print edition published by BBC Audiobooks Ltd, Bath, 2009.
Published by arrangement with the author.

U.K.Hardcover ISBN 978 1 408 42159 8
U.K.Softcover ISBN 978 1 408 42160 4

Printed and bound in Great Britain by
CPI Antony Rowe, Chippenham, Wiltshire

Moving In

At last! She was here! Jenny dipped her headlights and slowed down as she drove into the village of Cragley. Her heart was beating wildly. She was afraid she wouldn't recognise the place.

But everything was as she remembered it from the maps and satellite photographs she had studied on the Internet—the houses built around the village green; the brightly-lit pub on the corner; the church; the little Victorian school; the war memorial; the . . . There it was! Her new home! She saw the SOLD sign, slowed down and braked with a sigh of relief. She was here. At last. This really was it.

She parked the car, switched off the engine and the lights and sat for a moment in the dark, flexing her fingers, rotating her shoulders. It had been a long drive. She wondered how far behind her the furniture van would be. The men driving it would be as tired as she was, but at least there were two of them. They could have taken turns at the wheel.

She took her mobile phone from her bag and called the number that Jim, the elder of the removal men, had given her before they'd set off with her furniture.

'We'll be about another half-hour,' he told

her now.

She smiled as she switched off the phone. They'd made good time. Then she got out of the car and stood staring at her new home and place of business.

It was part of an old stone terrace dating from Victorian times. Shop on the ground floor. Two-storied flat upstairs—a maisonette, really. Walled garden at the rear. It had been a huge gamble buying a property via the Internet but . . . it was time she took some risks in life.

Her pulse quickened and she gave a little shiver of delight. This was hers now—all of it!

'Good evening!' a man called as he strolled past with his dog.

She returned his greeting, trying not to sound as surprised as she felt. Where she'd just come from people didn't speak to strangers in such a familiar way.

'Looks like rain,' the man added, letting his dog lead him on.

'Oh, dear! I hope not.'

She really did hope not. Not yet. Not tonight. Not until they got the van emptied. She shivered again, this time with apprehension, and walked slowly up to the front door to let herself inside.

* * *

She didn't bother looking inside the shop. She

2

headed straight upstairs to the flat. Her flat now. Her new home.

It was every bit as spacious as it had appeared on the website. More than big enough for her. She walked quickly from room to room.

They were big rooms with high ceilings. Three bedrooms, two reception rooms and a bathroom and kitchen. That was about it. But enough. More than enough for her.

The whole place needed re-decorating, of course. She'd known that. Otherwise, there wasn't much wrong with it. Hardly anything at all, in fact. She was delighted.

She was glad all the curtains and carpets had been left behind. They were well-worn and she wouldn't keep them long, but for now they were better than having bare floorboards and nothing over the windows. And the central heating system was new. Wonderful! She would get that on as soon as she could. Late August only, and not really cold, but the whole place felt chilly and damp from being empty for so long.

She stood in the middle of the living-room, twirled around and grinned. Her own place, at last. Exactly what she'd wanted. It was up to her now what she made of it.

'Hello!' a voice called up the stairs. 'Is there someone up there?'

The removal men!

'Coming!' she called back, heading for the

3

stairs.

The man standing in her hallway looking up at her as she ran down the stairs was tall with black, curly hair, and lots of it. Not a bit like either of the removal men.

'Oh, can I help you?' she asked in some confusion.

He looked equally puzzled.

'Err . . . I saw the door open and thought I'd better check the place wasn't being burgled or vandalised. Not that I can imagine there's anything in there to steal or spoil. The place has been empty so long. But you don't look like a burglar so I take it you must be the new owner?'

Before she had chance to reply he went on, 'And I take it that's your car outside?'

'The silver one? Yes. Is anything wrong?'

He shook his head. 'Not really, but people along here don't usually leave their cars at the front. We park around the back.'

'Oh, I'm sorry! I didn't realise.'

She stepped forward, edging him back towards the front steps and the pavement. She had no idea who he was, but she didn't like him standing on the threshold of her property as if he had some sort of right to be there.

'I'll need to move my car anyway,' she assured him. 'I'll need to clear the space for

4

the furniture van that's going to appear any minute now, with two big, strong men in it. Do you live round here?' she added quickly.

'Next door.'

'Oh?' That was something of a relief. She'd begun to worry about assault and mugging. 'Well, if we're neighbours, we should introduce ourselves. I'm Jenny Morrison.'

'Tom Laidler. So you're moving in this evening?'

'I am.'

'And what about the shop? What are you doing with that?'

'It's going to be a craft shop,' she announced proudly. 'I'll soon have it up and running.'

'A what? A craft shop?' He stared at her, as if incredulous.

'Yes.'

'Oh well, good luck with it. You'll doubtless need some. That shop's been all sorts of businesses. Butcher's, grocer's, shoe shop . . . never been a craft shop though. Hmm . . . from down south are you, from your accent?'

'Err . . . yes . . . Is that a problem?'

'Not for me. It might be for you though.'

Oh dear, she thought. Is this going to be one of those villages where they don't like strangers and hound out newcomers?

'Err . . . why might it be a problem for me?'

'Because summer's nearly over and it gets really cold and bleak up here in the winter.

5

You might find it hard going after being used to the weather down south. Ah! Here's your removal van now!' he announced, and then walked away to disappear through a door further along the pavement.

She grimaced. Not the friendliest of neighbours!

Then she stepped on to the pavement and waved to catch the van driver's attention.

* * *

The removal men were very helpful. Tired as they must have been, they got straight to work and everything was offloaded in an hour.

'You've got the rest of your life to sort it out,' Jim, the older man, pointed out as they stood together staring at the mountain of boxes in the kitchen.

'Yes,' she said vaguely.

'Will that be long enough, though?' Jason, the young one, asked mischievously.

Jenny laughed and rallied. 'Go away!' she said. 'You're just a young troublemaker.'

'He is,' Jim agreed. 'I keep telling him that.'

'Me? I'm innocent, me!'

'Why do I find that hard to believe?' she said with a chuckle. 'But you've done wonderfully well today,' she said. 'Both of you have been marvellous. What will you do now, though? Do you want to stay here overnight? I'm sure I can find extra bedding in one of

6

these boxes.'

Truthfully, she wasn't sure she could at all, but she didn't want the men dozing in their van after the day they'd just had.

Jim shook his head. 'Thanks all the same, but the office has booked us into a guest-house down the road a little way.'

'You are well-organised!'

He nodded. 'So, if you don't mind, we'll leave you to it and young Jason here can get some beauty sleep.'

'It's not me that's needing beauty sleep,' Jason pointed out indignantly. 'Have you looked in the mirror recently, Grandfather?'

'I take no notice of him,' Jim said with a wink.

Laughing, Jenny saw them to the door and watched them begin the first stage of their long journey back down south. It was as if the last link with Dartford, with her Mum and with her previous life, was broken. Now she really was on her own in a strange land.

'Welcome to Cragley!' called out a teenage girl who was passing by.

'Thank you!' Jenny replied with an answering smile.

'Think you'll survive up here, though?' asked the young boy who was following close behind the girl. 'It's a tough place for softie southerners!'

Sniggering, the two of them went into the same house that Tom Laidler had gone into

7

earlier.

Oh yes! she said to herself, trying to be strong after a moment of uncertainty. Yes, I will survive! The winter, and a lot more besides if I must. All my bridges are burned now.

New Neighbours

Surprisingly, Jenny slept well that first night. The sleep of exhaustion, perhaps, but she felt fresh and fully recovered when she awoke the next morning. And she knew instantly, and exactly, where she was. It was the start of the first day of the rest of her life!

She lay still for a while, getting used to the unfamiliar room.

Everywhere was chaos and clutter and boxes. And walls and a ceiling that were different. The window was in the wrong place, too. It certainly wasn't the house where she had spent nearly all her life. No roar of traffic bustling down the A2 either. In fact, she concluded with a wry smile, it wasn't Dartford at all. Whatever would Mum think?

Then she frowned and struggled with her emotions for a moment. She was used to Mum no longer being with her, but thinking of her and their life together still brought the threat of tears.

She threw the bed covers aside and sat up. Then she laughed. Bed covers! A couple of coats and some curtains! She'd been far too tired last night to hunt for bedding and had made do with whatever had come easily to hand.

Mum would have had a fit. She chuckled and shook her head. If Mum had been with her still, they would have had to spend the night in a B & B somewhere. Not that the need would ever have arisen. Leaving Dartford while Mum was alive—moving house even—would have been unthinkable. Totally impossible. Quite out of the question.

But that's enough of that! she decided. Things were different now. Time to make a start a new start.

*   *   *

Breakfast consisted of muesli and some long-life milk she'd kept carefully to hand and then, as soon as she'd eaten, she began sorting through her belongings. Much of the unpacking could wait but she did need stuff for the kitchen and the bathroom as a priority. Some clean clothes, too. And proper bedding.

Happily, the removal men had very kindly plugged in the fridge and the washing machine before they left. They had also put much of the furniture in the provisionally correct places. Not all of it, though. The big dresser was on the wrong wall, for a start. And the oak chest was in the wrong bedroom. But such things could wait. There were more urgent matters requiring attention.

After a couple of hours she decided she'd made a good enough start on sorting out her belongings and deserved a break. Besides, she was eager to take a look outside and get some fresh air. And she needed to buy some food. Time to see what the village shop was like. Tesco it wouldn't be, but that wasn't the end of the world. Just the world she knew.

*　　　*　　　*

The man from next door was standing on the pavement when she opened her front door.

'Good morning, Mr Laidler,' she said in a level tone.

He looked round at her and nodded. 'Good morning! So how are you getting on then? Have you unpacked yet?'

A wave of relief washed over her. It was a better start than she had feared after the previous evening's exchange.

'Not quite!' she said with a chuckle. 'But I've made a start.'

'Aye, well. It'll take you a while.'

They spoke then about the weather, and how warm it still was for the time of year. Jenny was happy with that. At least there was no mention of terrible winters and how would

10

she survive with her soft, southern ways!

'If you want a hand with anything,' Tom said eventually, 'just ask. I'm never far away.' He seemed a different person. It was hard to understand.

'Thank you,' Jenny said. She hesitated. 'I'm just going to the village shop but I might take you up on your offer later, if I may. There are a couple of pieces of furniture I probably couldn't move on my own.'

'No problem,' he assured her. 'Look, I'm sorry about last night. I feel we got off on the wrong foot. My fault entirely. I was feeling really scratchy. Yesterday was a bad day for me.'

'Don't worry about it,' she told him cheerfully. 'We all have those.'

*   *   *

'Are you here on holiday?' the woman in the shop wanted to know.

Jenny shook her head. 'No.' She took a deep breath and added, 'I've just moved in.'

The woman paused from ringing things up on the till. 'Oh? To live, you mean?'

'That's right.'

'And where is it you've moved into?' She looked puzzled.

'Providence Lane. Just across the green.'

'Oh! The old shop?'

'That's right.'

11

'I didn't know anyone had moved in there. I heard it had been sold, of course, but . . .'

'Last night,' Jenny said. 'I moved in last night—late.'

The woman smiled. 'I'm Wendy, Wendy Rogers, by the way. Welcome to Cragley! I hope you like it here.'

'Thank you.'

Jenny introduced herself 'Is this your own shop?' she added.

'Yes, it is. Not exactly a goldmine but somehow we keep going. What about your shop? What are you going to do with that? Convert it back into part of the house?'

Jenny outlined her plan.

'Oh? That sounds lovely. Cragley could do with something like that. It will bring some visitors in.'

Just as Jenny began to feel pleased, a voice from behind her said, 'It'll never work, something like that. Not in Cragley. What we need is a computer shop. Something modern and useful, not something else for the dinosaurs!'

It was the boy from next door. He was standing in the doorway, hands deep in his pockets, looking belligerent.

'What do you know?' Wendy scoffed. 'When you've done a day's work, James, folk might begin to listen to you. Until then . . .'

Jenny turned away, discomfited by the unpleasantness. She felt the boy staring at her,

12

challenging her to say something. She gave Wendy a vague smile and headed for the door.

'Bye, now!' Wendy called after her. 'See you again.'

Jenny responded but her mind was on other things. What an unpleasant young man, she thought. He would have to live next door to me!

Settling In

When she got back indoors, Jenny finally got round to having a look around the shop. There was dust everywhere, and collapsed shelving with brackets torn from the wall. It was hard to see what sort of shop it had once been.

A dress shop, she'd been told when she'd made her offer for it. Or a shoe shop. Something like that. But it was just a mess now. Someone had even squirted a rude message on the window and although she wanted to be fair-minded, the youth next door seemed a likely culprit.

She rubbed off the message and stood back. There was a lot to do and she began to feel a bit daunted. But she would sort out the flat first, she reminded herself. There would be plenty of time to get round to the shop. It was going to take her a while to get that organised.

Already, though, she could see her future plans for the shop taking shape in her mind's eye. It was a decent size. The display area occupied only part of the ground floor of the building. About two-thirds of it. In the remainder there was a storage room, a toilet and even a small kitchen. So it was self-contained. Excellent, she thought with satisfaction. Perfect. Just what she wanted.

A knock at the door distracted her. It was her neighbour, Tom Laidler.

'Busy?' he asked.

'Not really. I'm just sorting out in my mind what needs to be done with the shop.'

'Plenty, I daresay. The place has been empty for a while. I saw you in here and I wondered when you wanted a hand with moving your furniture?' he added.

'Oh, yes! Thank you. What about now?'

'Now would be great. I need to get over to Berwick when we're done here.'

'Berwick-on-Tweed? Do you go there a lot?'

'It's the nearest town. So, yes, I suppose I do. You can't get everything you need here in Cragley.'

She laughed. 'Hardly anything, in fact!'

'That's just about right. At one time this village had most things you needed, but not now. The bank closed. The Co-op closed. You can't even get petrol here now, and I don't know how long the post office will last. You can still go to church, though—just about. There's not even a permanent minister any more.'

'Oh? I hadn't realised things were as bad as that.'

'You soon will. Then you might change your mind about living here. The back of beyond, Cragley is these days. There were more services and facilities here in Victorian times.'

Such pessimism, she thought wryly. She didn't think she could be doing with seeing a lot of Tom Laidler. She preferred people who saw the glass as half-full, not half-empty.

*　　*　　*

'A cup of coffee?' she asked when they had finished moving the big items of furniture.

'Oh, I don't . . .'

'I can manage that, just about.' She waved a hand at the mess. 'Tea, no. I don't know where it is. But I've found the coffee.'

'Aye, all right, then.'

He sat down.

She picked up the kettle.

'Have you lived here long?'

He smiled. 'Most of my life, I suppose.'

'So you must know what the shop downstairs used to be. The estate agent wasn't sure.'

'You name it. It's been everything, in its time. Last, it was a kiddies' clothing shop. But

15

before that . . . shoes, souvenirs, outdoor clothing, estate agent's office, provision merchant . . .' He paused and grinned. 'But it's never been a craft shop—not in my lifetime.'

She laughed. 'Everything else, though!'

'Aye. I even had ideas for it myself.'

'Oh? What as?'

He stretched and yawned. 'It doesn't matter now. That time has gone.'

She accepted the closure and changed tack. 'Are they your children, by the way, the young boy and girl that I've seen going in your front door?'

'Probably. James and Hannah they're called.'

'How old are they?'

'Fifteen.'

'Both? Oh! So they're . . .'

'Twins, yes.' He nodded and looked away.

He didn't volunteer any more information about them, and she didn't ask.

'How about you?' he asked. 'Any family?'

She shook her head. 'There's just me.'

She almost added, *now,* but she didn't. She said nothing about how until recently there had been her mother, too. She had to get used to being a truly single person.

'It's a big house for just one person?' he suggested.

'I suppose it is, yes. But I wanted somewhere with plenty of room—and with a shop.'

16

'A craft shop,' he said again, with that crooked smile.

'What's wrong with that?' she asked, slightly flustered.

'Nothing. Nothing at all.' He glanced at his watch. 'I must be going. Thanks for the coffee.'

'Thank you for your help.'

On the way out, he turned and said, 'If the kids give you any hassle, let me know. They're not bad kids, but . . .'

He said no more and went on his way.

She wasn't sure what to make of his comment. What sort of hassle did he think his children were going to give her?

But after he'd gone she had too much to do to wonder about it for long.

*   *   *

One day in the village shop, Wendy introduced Jenny to the local joiner, Harry Cummings, who she said would be able to help with the alterations and fittings for the gift shop. But as soon as she started to speak to him, Jenny had doubts. It wasn't so much that he seemed disinterested. He was simply very busy.

'It'll be a while before I can get round to you,' he said. 'I've got a lot of work on at the minute.'

'That's all right, Mr Cummings. I've got plenty of clearing up to do first anyway.'

17

'Aye. You'd best order a skip. That old place will be full of stuff to get rid of.'

It was good advice. While she was pondering it, the shop doorbell rang and another customer came in. The newcomer was a youngish man with a goatee beard and a twinkle in his eye.

'Morning, Harry!' he called, managing to give Jenny a smile at the same time.

Harry looked dubious. 'Morning,' he muttered back.

'So when are you coming to mend my roof?'

'As soon as I can, Mr Renfrew. Just as soon as I can.'

'Winter's coming on, Harry,' the newcomer added, with a wink at Jenny. 'Rain and snow on the way. Icy winds. Frost. The lot! I'm relying on you to get the job done as soon as possible.'

'Join the queue!' Harry told him. 'And it's a long one.'

'And is this young lady part of it?' the younger man murmured, turning to Jenny with an engaging smile. 'Will Renfrew,' he offered, somehow managing to give the impression he was doffing a top hat to her. 'Artist.'

She smiled and shook his outstretched hand.

'Really? A shopkeeper?' he queried, when she had introduced herself.

'Not quite yet, but I hope to be. Intend to be,' she corrected herself.

'She's in your line of business, Mr Renfrew,' Harry intervened mournfully.

'Oh?'

'Not exactly,' Jenny said hastily. 'I'm not an artist myself. But I'm going to open a craft shop.'

'Ah! Really? Excellent. Just what Cragley needs.'

'You're the second person to say that.'

'Cragley would be better off with a petrol pump,' Harry suggested darkly.

'Now, Harry!' Will Renfrew wagged a finger in admonishment. 'That's a tad ungracious. A craft shop will be a definite enhancement to Cragley.'

Somehow Jenny ended up going for coffee with Will Renfrew in a nearby tea shop.

'Are you really an artist?' she asked.

He nodded. 'Not world-famous, though— yet!' he added, with a disarming smile.

'A painter?'

He nodded.

'What do you paint?'

'The ruined castle mostly.'

'The?'

'The village's most prized possession. It puts us on the tourist map. But I also paint dog and cat portraits. Occasionally a child, although I'm not so keen on the children.'

'Why ever not?'

'They're very noisy, they won't sit still, and they throw things at me. More coffee?'

19

So Much To Do!

Over the next few days Jenny made a good start at clearing up the shop. The flat was in reasonably good order but the shop was truly derelict. Whatever had not been wanted had been dumped there, and what was already there had been left to decay and disintegrate. The advice to order a skip was good. She took it, and soon after the skip arrived she had it almost filled. But anything that might conceivably be useful or of value, she took down to the big, empty shed at the bottom of the garden.

Once the shop was clear, she swept the floor and gave it a good wash. Beneath the plaster dust and the sawdust, she was delighted to find ornate Victorian tiling, with only one or two tiles missing. She was also pleased to see that previous occupants had not ripped out the original cast-iron fireplace with its tiled surround. She could make a feature of that.

*　　　*　　　*

On one of her return journeys from the shed, she saw Hannah, the girl next-door, sitting astride the party wall that ran between their gardens. Before she could call a greeting, the girl spoke to her.

'What are you doing that for? Taking all that stuff down there?'

'I'm clearing out the old shop, Hannah.'

The girl nodded without much interest. 'How long are you staying?' she asked.

'Staying? I'm not sure I know what you mean.'

'In this house—in Cragley!'

'Well . . .' Jenny was stumped for a moment. She wasn't sure how to respond. 'It's my home now, Hannah.'

The girl seemed slightly more interested. 'The last people only stayed three months,' she said.

'Well, I hope to stay a lot longer than that.'

'But what will you do for money?'

Jenny smiled to herself at the surprisingly pragmatic question.

'I'm going to re-open the shop. It's going to be a craft shop. Didn't your dad tell you?'

Hannah shook her head. 'He doesn't say much to me. In fact, I don't think he likes me very much. I'm just a girl. He prefers James.'

'No, of course he doesn't! Fathers aren't like that. They don't have favourites amongst their children. Anyway, they all love their daughters.'

'Mine doesn't.'

'I'm sure he does.'

'You don't know him!' Hannah called, sliding down from her perch and out of sight

21

on the other side of the wall.

Jenny smiled wryly to herself as she headed back to the house. There's a bit of teenage insecurity there, she thought, unless I'm very much mistaken.

*   *   *

With the clearing-up done in the shop, she waited with mounting impatience for the joiner to come and begin tackling the alterations she'd discussed with him.

After a few days she dropped by Harry Cummings' workshop to remind him, but received little encouragement.

'I'll not be long now,' he assured her in a tone of voice that implied the very opposite.

*   *   *

Jenny decided to turn her attention to the garden and began clearing that up.

She also began to peruse her collection of trade catalogues and started ordering items she wanted to stock in the shop. Some things would probably take a long time to arrive, so she might as well make a start on building up her range of stock now.

One afternoon as she was daydreaming over a catalogue of exquisite hand-made silk flowers, she was startled by the unmistakable sound of glass breaking somewhere at the back of the house. She jumped up with a start and ran to investigate.

She might have known, she thought bitterly. The twins!

Recently there hadn't been a day that had gone by without something happening, something they'd done to annoy her deliberately, something she could have done without.

Now they were sitting once more on the wall that divided the two gardens, throwing stones at whatever took their eye including the old greenhouse in her garden.

'James! Hannah! What on earth are you doing? Stop it! I want to use the greenhouse.'

'That old thing?' James said scornfully. 'It's neither use nor ornament.'

'It's mine,' she responded firmly, 'whatever you think of it. And I don't want you throwing stones at it. I don't want you throwing stones at anything else in my garden either.'

'Garden?' Hannah said with an eerie laugh, more a cackle. 'Call this dump a garden?'

James laughed in support.

Jenny stood firm. 'I mean what I say,' she said. Just for emphasis, she added pointedly, 'I had hoped I would have good neighbours when I moved here.'

'Well, what you've got is us!' James responded. With a raucous laugh, he jumped off the wall and disappeared from view.

Hannah followed a moment or two later,

having given Jenny a cool stare that was even more troubling.

*　　*　　*

Jenny walked down the garden and surveyed the greenhouse. There were quite a few panes missing, most of them no doubt having disappeared long ago. All the same . . . She wondered how many of the missing panes were down to the twins.

She opened the door with difficulty and gazed inside. Lots of broken glass on the floor. Some rotten wood and cobwebbed metal.

The soft September wind whistled through the gaps left by the missing panes. Even so, the greenhouse was still standing, so perhaps the structure was sound. And it was nice and big. She could grow tomatoes and salad crops in here, if nothing else, once she got round to it. Next year, say. In the spring.

Provided the twins hadn't destroyed it totally by then!

She sighed. What a family! There was something wrong —something worrying about the whole lot of them. She wondered what it was. She also wondered about the lady of the house. She had seen nothing of her. In fact, she was beginning to wonder if there was one.

The father, Tom, could be pleasant enough on a good day, but his children . . .

24

She hadn't expected to find children behaving as they did in this part of the world. She'd thought of Northumberland as a place of refuge from the modern world and its problems. She hoped she hadn't got that entirely wrong.

A Talk With Tom

When Jenny next saw Tom Laidler she took the opportunity to have a word with him about the twins and their attitude towards her. She tried to be diplomatic and not make it a full-on complaint, but he saw through that and was instantly defensive.

'There's nothing wrong with them,' he said defiantly. 'They're grand kids.'

'Of course they are! I didn't say there was anything wrong with them. It's just that some of the things they do and say are a bit . . . well, a bit upsetting, to be honest. I was hoping you might have a word with them.'

'The trouble with people around here is they all want to live your life for you. They want everyone to live just like them.'

'That's not the point, Tom.'

'And they're a bunch of old fuddy-duddies. They forget what they were like themselves at that age. Fifteen is a difficult age, nowadays more than ever.'

This wasn't the conversation she had anticipated, she thought with something approaching despair. It was like fighting your way through sheets of clingfilm.

'Tom, can you just calm down for a minute? Please!'

He looked at her with suspicion. 'I know what you're going to say,' he insisted. 'You're going to go on about how they should be in school!'

'Tom, the main thing I wanted to ask you to do was to stop them sitting on the garden wall and throwing stones at my greenhouse breaking the glass and then being cheeky about it when I ask them to stop.'

He snorted and shook his head. 'Is that all?'

'It isn't, actually, no. But it's enough, isn't it?' She was nettled by his attitude and added, 'Any more of it, and I'm going to send you the bill for repairs. How does that grab you? And if that doesn't stop them, I shall report them to the police.'

He sighed wearily. 'The police know all about them. You'll not be telling them anything new.'

'But you will speak to Hannah and James?'

He nodded. 'Aye, I expect so.'

'Come and have a coffee with me, Tom,' she suggested, relenting, anxious to reach happier ground. 'You can see what I'm doing with the shop. Give me some advice, maybe.'

He hesitated, but not for long. She sensed

he, too, was eager to change the subject.

* * *

'I see you've got most of the boxes unpacked and put away,' he said, as she showed him into the kitchen.
'Oh, that was the easy bit. The shop and the garden are the big challenges.'
Tactfully, she didn't mention the word greenhouse again. She didn't mention the twins again either. She wanted to calm things down and take the heat out of the situation.
He sat down at the table and waited in silence while she made two cups of coffee.
'Would you like a biscuit? They're not chocolate ones, I'm afraid. I've eaten all those, it's just the horrible plain ones that are left in the tin.'
'Well, don't you go buying any more until you've finished those.'
She grinned. 'You sound just like my mother! Where did that come from?'
'From my mother, probably. Did yours go on about the starving millions in Africa, if you didn't eat everything on your plate?'
She nodded. 'Two of a kind, eh? I wonder if they've still got the mould.'
'I don't think so. Haven't we got an obesity problem now?' He laughed, in a gentle way that started somewhere deep down and gradually found its way to the surface, until in

the end he couldn't keep it quiet any longer. And Jenny found herself shaking her head, and spluttering and laughing with him. 'Anyway,' she said, when she recovered, 'when the shop's open for business, I'll serve coffee to the customers—for free.'

'Nice. Fancy ideas,' he added with a grin.

She pulled a face. 'Customer friendly, that's all. I want the place to be warm and welcoming, and I want people to be eager to come inside.'

'Do you think you'll get any?'

'What? Customers?'

He nodded.

'I hope so! And I hope they'll be coming into my shop to spend some money! Not just to get a free cup of coffee!'

He laughed again and said, 'It'll go down a treat, free coffee. They'll be coming from as far away as Edinburgh and Newcastle for that.'

She smiled and felt relieved. They seemed more relaxed with one another now. She was glad.

'About the twins,' he said suddenly.

She waited.

'They can be difficult, I know. None better. But they're not so bad, really.'

'I know that,' she said gently. 'They're not bank robbers or serial killers, or anything, are they? They just like helping my old greenhouse to collapse.'

28

He smiled and dipped his head. 'I'm sorry, Jenny, if they've been giving you a hard time.'

'I just wanted you to have a word with them. That's all. Nip things in the bud before they get out of hand.'

'I will. I'll do that.'

She sipped her coffee and tried not to study his face. She didn't want him to feel under interrogation. She didn't want him to clam up again.

'It's been difficult,' he said. 'Ever since their mother died, it's been an uphill struggle.'

Ah! She'd wondered about the mother. Here was the answer. 'I'm sorry to hear that, Tom. What happened?'

'Annie got ill.' He shrugged and added, 'That's all, really. She passed away after a short illness, as they say. It broke my heart. I was devastated. The twins were, as well.'

'You must all have been. How long ago was it?'

'Three years gone. Nearly four now.'

'You must all have had a terrible time,' she said gently. 'I can see that. How awful for you. And the poor children.'

He looked up and gave a weary smile. 'It's not what we planned, Annie and me. We were a happy family once. But things happen. You just have to get on with it, don't you?'

True enough.

She offered him another coffee, but the mood had changed and he declined.

'They won't go to school, you know.'

'The twins? Why ever not?'

He shook his head. 'They just won't. The battles we've had over that! I used to have to see them on to the school bus or they wouldn't have bothered getting on. But all that meant was that they got off at the next stop and spent the day roaming round the countryside. I decided I'd rather have them here all day instead. But that meant I had to give up my job. I probably would have had to, anyway,' he added. 'I wasn't up to it any more.'

'Was the Education Authority happy with that arrangement?'

He shook his head. 'But they accepted it.'

'Really? I thought it was the law that children had to go to school?'

'It's not so unusual, apparently. I was told there are a lot of kids around here—lads, especially—who give up on school when they're fourteen or fifteen. Out on the farms. Isolated places in the hills. The authorities don't like it, but . . .' He shrugged. 'Nobody has the answer.'

Jenny was surprised. She had assumed truancy was a problem only in the inner cities, the world she knew best.

'What was your job, Tom?' she asked to change the subject.

'Joiner and carpenter.'

'Really? Like Harry Cummings?'

'No,' he said with a shake of his head. 'Not

like him at all. He's a joiner and boat builder. It says so on his door!'

'Ah! Big difference.'

'It is. Not that he gets the chance to build many boats. When's he coming to do this work for you?'

'I haven't a clue. I don't think he has either. He's snowed under with work.'

Tom nodded and said, 'He's not much for the joinery, anyway. He's a boat builder at heart.'

'But where would you use a boat around here?' she said wonderingly, thinking about it. 'On the river?'

'On the Tweed,' Tom agreed, looking up with a smile. 'For the fishing, you know.'

Hannah Says Sorry

'Is this shop still not open?' She spun round and smiled at Will Renfrew who was standing on the threshold, rattling the defunct door handle.

'Soon!' she told him. 'It will be open very soon, I hope. And how are you today, Will?'

'Excellent, thank you. And a very good morning to you, too, my dear,' he responded, doffing an imaginary hat.

She had been cleaning the inside of the shop window. Now she dropped the cloth into the bucket and began to unpeel the yellow rubber gloves she was wearing.

'I'm a bit frustrated, to be honest, Will,' she told him. 'I'd hoped to be up and running by now.' She waved a despairing hand at the shop front and added, 'But I'm not.'

'These things take time,' he said soothingly. 'Give yourself a break. Come and join me in The Leaping Salmon.'

'The pub? Is that where you're headed?'

'It is.'

'Now? At this time of day?'

'I've just won a commission. I'm celebrating.'

'Still . . . It's only ten in the morning, Will.'

'For coffee, I should have said. Just for coffee.'

'In the pub?'

'That's their morning trade. Den of iniquity at night, I'm told, but in the morning it's highly respectable.'

'Respectable?' she repeated dubiously, looking him up and down, assessing his paint-spattered cord trousers and old jumper.

'You'll do,' he assured her. 'Just come as you are.'

'Thank you very much! Is that your artist's attire, by the way?'

'My gardening attire.'

'Think they'll let you in, dressed like that?'

'I'll tell them I'm going to pay cash.'

'For the coffee?'

32

'Heaven save me from petty shopkeepers! Are you ever going to get your coat?'

* * *

'So what's the problem with getting your shop opened?' Will asked when they were safely inside The Leaping Salmon. She hesitated and surveyed her surroundings. 'I've not been in here before,' she said, eyeing the surprisingly fresh décor. 'It's quite nice, isn't it?'

'Not bad now smoking's banned and they can keep the place clean.'

'And you were right about the morning clientele. Very respectable!'

There were half-a-dozen elderly people enjoying morning coffee while they chatted or read their newspapers.

'The shop,' Will said firmly. 'What's the problem?'

She smiled at him. 'You're very persistent.'

'I am. Indeed I am.'

Handsome, too, in a Johnny Deppish way, she thought with amusement. She wasn't keen on the little beard but it certainly added to his aura. He shouldn't be here, though. He should be in Vienna or Prague, in the 1890's. He should be wearing a hat and carrying a cane or an umbrella, an elegant lady by his side.

'My patience is not unlimited,' he warned her.

She laughed and put down her coffee cup.

'The problem is Harry Cummings, the joiner. I'm still waiting for him to do various repairs and alterations and to put up the shelves. I can't open for business until that's done.'

'Well, if he comes to fit-up your shop before he fixes my leaking roof, I shall be furious.'

'Oh, dear! Of course. You've been waiting some time for him to get round to doing a job for you as well, haven't you?'

'Only for a year.'

'A year!'

'Just over, actually. But that's not long. Not for around here, it isn't. Besides, the roof has probably been leaking for most of the last century.'

'Is your house in poor repair?'

'Not at all. At least, I don't think so. But when my grandfather designed it, he clearly specified the kind of buckets to be put under the leaks. It's just that you can't get them any more. So the roof will have to be mended instead.'

'I see.' She laughed and shook her head.

'But I must be going,' he said, glancing at the old clock on the wall. 'I must make a start on my latest commission.'

'What is it?'

'A family portrait. Three cocker spaniels and a Persian cat.'

She shook her head again, and tried not to

laugh.

'About your problem,' he said, standing up and helping Jenny to her feet.

'My problem?'

'With the shop. You could do worse than ditch Harry Cummings and approach your next-door neighbour to do the work.'

'Tom Laidler?'

'That's him.' Will nodded. 'He's an excellent joiner. At least, he was. I know he hasn't worked for a while, but I don't suppose he's forgotten how.'

She nodded thoughtfully. It was an idea.

'One other thing.'

She waited.

'Would you care to come here with me one evening for a meal? Local salmon—cooked, not leaping—or whatever else takes your fancy?'

'I'd like that very much,' she assured him, overcoming her surprise. 'Thank you, Will.'

*   *   *

Back at the house, Jenny found she had a surprise visitor waiting for her. 'Hello, Hannah! Are you looking for me?'

The girl nodded. 'You weren't in though. So I waited.'

'So are you coming inside?' Jenny asked, opening the door. Hannah looked uncertain.

'Come and have a cup of coffee with me. Or

35

tea? Or whatever else we can find.'

'I just wanted to say sorry about the greenhouse,' Hannah said in a rush. 'That's all.'

'Oh? Has your dad had a word with you?'

The girl nodded.

Jenny smiled. 'Well, thank you for that, Hannah. I'm glad you came. I know it's just an old wreck of a greenhouse at the moment, but as I told your dad I want to repair it and use it. But come on in, Hannah! Let's have a drink and a chat. If you've got time?'

Hannah grinned with what seemed like relief and nodded.

The ice seemed to be broken at last, Jenny thought with relief as she ushered the girl inside.

Hannah wasn't much of a chatterbox but she did speak and listen normally when they reached the kitchen, like a grown-up young woman instead of a difficult child. Jenny welcomed the change.

'You're making it nice in here.' Hannah looked round the kitchen with interest.

'Well, I've made a start. I've decorated the kitchen and one of the bedrooms.'

'Yourself?'

Jenny nodded. 'Of course.'

'I like painting—painting walls, that is.'

'Oh, I don't do pictures either.'

Hannah grinned. 'My mum used to like decorating. I do, as well. But Dad says our house is all right as it is. So I don't get the chance now.'

'Come and help me do some of mine,' Jenny said quickly.

'Maybe.' Hannah considered. Then she said, 'I saw you going into the pub with Mr Renfrew.'

'Did you? We just went for a coffee. It's quite a nice place.'

'Old-fashioned,' Hannah said quickly. 'It's where the old people go.'

'Thank you, Hannah.'

The girl smiled but took nothing back.

That puts me in my place! Jenny thought wryly.

'You know Mr Renfrew, do you, Hannah?'

'Yes. He used to be the art teacher at my school.'

When you and James used to go to school, presumably, Jenny thought but didn't say.

'He likes painting, as well—but not walls,' Jenny said mischievously.

'That's all he does now,' Hannah said in a serious tone. 'Paint pictures. He left the school.'

'Perhaps he got bored with it?'

'Probably he did.' Hannah got to her feet. 'Where do you want painting?'

'Another bedroom is next on the list.'

'Where's the paint?'

'What, now?' Jenny asked with alarm.

Hannah nodded. She was ready to start.

37

Well, why not? Jenny thought, trying to recall the old saying of her mother's about striking while the iron was hotor something like that.

*   *   *

Hannah made a fair job of it, too. 'Very good!' Jenny said with admiration when she came to inspect the end result.
'Hmm. I think I've done better,' Hannah responded self-critically. 'But I'm a bit out of practice so I'm sure to improve.'
Just then a voice called to her from downstairs.
'That's James looking for me!' Hannah said, putting down the paint roller. 'I have to go.'
Jenny thanked her and invited her to come again. They descended the stairs together to find James waiting on the front steps.
'What have you been doing?' he asked, staring at his sister suspiciously.
'Painting,' Hannah told him.
'Painting?'
'Painting bedroom walls,' Jenny said. 'You could have a go as well, if you like, James. There's plenty wants doing.'
James looked disgusted.
'Or how about helping me clear up the greenhouse?' Jenny suggested. 'All that broken glass?'
James grimaced, and turned and marched
38

off. Hannah followed, without a backward glance.

'Come again, Hannah!' Jenny called. 'Any time.'

She got a little wave and a smile from Hannah then, but nothing at all from James. Still, she thought as she headed indoors, one out of two ain't bad. Two out of three, actually, if you counted Tom as well. Progress!

A Dinner Date

Wendy in the village shop asked Jenny how she was getting along.

'Still settling in, but I'm fine, thanks.'

'There'll be a lot to do. It's years since that shop was last open. Even longer since it was a success story.'

'Oh, I haven't even started on the shop yet. I'm still waiting for the joiner to come and do some work on it'

'Harry Cummings?'

'That's him. You recommended him, remember?'

Wendy winced. Then she chuckled. 'Has he said which year he'll come?'

'Not yet,' Jenny replied with a weary smile. 'He's very busy, isn't he?'

'He is. He's good, mind. But he can be hard to get hold of.' She began scanning the items

39

in Jenny's basket.

'I see you've got some new technology.'

'The scanner?' Wendy chuckled. 'It's all right but I'm not sure it's justified in my little shop. What I really need are more customers.'

'Was it expensive to install the scanner?'

'Not for me. It came free—from One North East, the regional development agency. So I thought I might as well have it. They have a grant programme to support rural shops. Money from Brussels, I think. You might want to look into it yourself.'

'Oh, I don't think so. I won't have anything like as many customers as you, Wendy. Everybody has to buy bread and milk, don't they? But you don't need to buy scented candles and hand-crafted paper.'

'True enough. Still, One North East might be able to help you in some other way.'

'You're right. I'll look into it.'

'Ten pounds and forty-three pence, please,' Wendy concluded.

While Jenny counted out the money, getting rid of some small change in the process, Wendy added, 'You should have told Harry Cummings you wanted a boat built. He'd have been round like a shot!'

'You're not the first to put that idea in my head.'

'Well, if you can't wait any longer, have a word with Tom Laidler, your next-door neighbour. He's a joiner. Used to be, anyway.'

40

'Someone else suggested that as well. But it's a bit awkward. I don't think he works now, does he?'

Wendy sighed. 'Not since Annie died, poor man. But he'll have to start again sometime, won't he? He can't go the rest of his life without working.'

'He says he has to look after the twins.'

'Well, he's a good man, is Tom, and I wouldn't question his motives. He's certainly got his hands full with the two of them, but those kids are growing up and it's time he pulled himself together and got on with his life. He's just going to waste.'

'You knew his wife?'

'I've known both of them all my life. Annie was lovely. So is Tom, actually. Annie wouldn't want to see him like this. He's turned into such a curmudgeon. It's such a shame.'

'The children seem to be difficult too.'

'That they are! But they're not bad kids. They get into scrapes, but they're teenagers. What can you expect? They miss their mum. That's the top and the bottom of it.'

'Tom says they won't go to school.'

'Well, maybe they won't, but they're not the only ones. It's a long way to the high school in Berwick every morning by school bus. Then they have a terrible time if they miss the bus when it's time to come home. It's not a nice experience. Anyway, the twins will be leaving next summer. I don't suppose either of them wants to stop on,' Wendy added.

Jenny picked up her bag. Then she paused. 'But you think Tom might help me out?'

'He might. It's worth a try.' Wendy grinned and added, 'Say I suggested it. The worst he can do is bite your head off!'

*   *   *

Will Renfrew was good company, Jenny decided with a happy smile as she sat down. On the way into The Leaping Salmon he'd found something pleasant or amusing to say to everyone they'd passed.

'Do you know absolutely everyone in this village?' she asked with a chuckle.

'Just about. What would you like to drink?'

'Lime and soda would be nice. And I'll have a glass of white wine with the meal, if I may.'

After their orders were sorted out, she said, 'Have you lived here a long time, Will?'

'All my life, apart from the years I was at art school.'

'Really? Never felt the urge to move on?'

He shook his head. 'Not really. Cragley suits me fine. Besides, there's a lot to be said for getting to know a place, really getting to know it.'

'And it takes a lifetime?'

'Seems to.'

They smiled at one another. Jenny wondered when she had last met such a

happy, contented man. Never, probably.
'What about you?' he asked. 'Where are
you from?'
'Nowhere much. Nowhere in particular.
Moved around a lot, I suppose, but always
around London. The last few years I mostly
looked after Mum in Dartford.'
'Never married?'
'No.'
'Me neither. But there's still plenty of time
for you.'
'Oh, I don't know about that!' Jenny
laughed. 'My friends seem to think I'm an old
maid now I've turned thirty. And I doubt I'll
ever find someone to suit me'
'Hard to please, eh?'
'Very. And too independent! Anyway,' she
added, changing the subject, 'Mum's gone
now. I still miss her terribly, but I had to
decide what to do with the rest of my life.'
'And this is it? A craft shop?'
She smiled. 'I hope so. I've always been
interested in craftwork, and the kind of art
that isn't . . . well, that isn't difficult, if you
know what I mean?'
'Not pickled sharks? Or somebody's
unmade bed?'
She laughed. 'No, not things like that at all!
I don't need controversy in my life. Or
political statements, or ugliness. None of that.
I like things of beauty, things that make me
feel happy and full of wonder. I'm a very

43

simple, straightforward sort of person, I suppose, and that doesn't trouble me. I'm happy with myself.'

Will weighed her words carefully and frowned. He was quiet for a moment. Then he said, 'But Cragley? Why Cragley? I know it's a perfectly charming little place—I ought to, after all—but even so . . .'

'I found it on the internet.'

He stared at her.

'I did searches. Googled for suitable properties and places. Looking for somewhere like this became a hobby. It's what I would do. Every evening for months after Mum died. It was a delicious game I would play when I came home from work to an empty house.

'I found Cragley, and as soon as I saw it, I knew the flat and shop were just what I wanted.'

'Really? Just like that?' Will shook his head and stared at her with apparent admiration. 'You're a gambler.'

She smiled and wondered if that was true. 'Desperate, more like it. Desperate to get on with my life.'

'Have you done anything like this before?'

'Opened a craft shop? No, of course not. I worked in a bank.' She laughed when she saw the look of surprise on his face. 'It's very brave of you,' he managed.

'Adventurous, you mean?'

'I suppose I do, yes. What happens if it goes

wrong?'

'I shall probably be very upset.'

'And throw things?'

'Possibly.'

They grinned at each other.

'I suppose it is a little risky,' she admitted.

'You didn't rob the bank before you left?'

'I thought about it. But somehow it wasn't me. I couldn't find the right mask to wear so I just had to give up the idea.'

He laughed and shook his head. 'So?' he insisted.

'So in the end I sold Mum's house instead and raised the money that way.'

'Chickened out of becoming a career bank robber!'

She nodded.

'Well,' he said, 'unlike you, I've never been able to bring myself to sell the parental home. My parents couldn't either.'

'So you live in your grandparents' house, just as your parents did before you?'

'That's right. On my own, too. I just rattle around in the place.'

That seemed sad. She took notice. Like her, then, he was on his own.

'There's still time for you, too, Will.'

He looked at her and gave a wry smile. 'Forty is no longer a distant horizon for me. It's approaching fast.'

'Still time to sell the house and see the world.'

'I suppose that's true, but I'm not terribly interested, to be honest. The only thing I've ever really wanted to do is paint.'

'Family portraits?'

'No. Those I do for a living.'

'What do you prefer to paint?'

'Come and see for yourself sometime. Come up to the house.'

She smiled and said, 'I'd like that.'

*　　　*　　　*

Later, she rang her friend Lucy, who lived back in Kent.

'Jenny! What a lovely surprise. How are you?'

Lucy stopped, considered and then added, 'What's wrong? Something's wrong, isn't it?'

Jenny laughed. 'Nothing! Absolutely nothing. Lucy, I know it's late but I had to tell you. I've just been out for a meal with a lovely man.'

'Really? Tell me more. I insist.'

'Well, he's an artist, and . . .'

'An artist? Oh, heaven! How absolutely perfect!'

Jenny thought she wouldn't go that far, but Will Renfrew was certainly a lovely surprise. She couldn't deny it. She didn't even want to try.

A Visit To Tweed House

Tom wasn't at all enthusiastic about helping Jenny with the shop repairs and refit. 'I don't have the time,' he said.

'No? It is a big job, I suppose. That will be why Harry Cummings hasn't been yet.'

'He still hasn't been?'

Jenny shook her head.

'Well, it'll be a good while now before he shows up. He's just started building a coble for a man from Tweedmouth'

'Oh? He's got a boat to build, has he?'

'At last. He's over the moon.'

'In that case I really will have to look for another joiner,' she said with disappointment. 'I've been waiting long enough.' She turned to make her way back inside the house.

'Have you seen Hannah?' Tom called after her.

'She's helping me in the kitchen.'

'Helping you? Hannah?'

'Yes, Tom. Helping me.'

It wasn't literally true. Hannah wasn't actually helping at that very moment, but she had been. Earlier they had finished decorating the last of the bedrooms together. Now Hannah was perusing some of Jenny's trade catalogues. She was interested in seeing what might be available for the shop.

47

'I like these candles,' she said, looking up as Jenny came into the kitchen. 'They're beeswax. That means they won't smell, doesn't it?'

'Not of wax, and they won't be smoky. They'll be nicely scented.'

Hannah considered the photographs. 'I like the shapes,' she decided. 'Big and chunky. I'm tired of skinny candles. They're all you ever see.'

'The ones you're looking at are church candles.'

'Are they? Will you order some?'

'Will they sell? That's the question? What do you think?'

Hannah shrugged. 'There're plenty of churches around here. They might.'

Jenny smiled. 'Let's order some then.'

'And you can see how they go?' Hannah suggested.

'Right.' Jenny hid another smile that was threatening to appear. 'Why don't you do the order, Hannah? Do it online. Do you know how?'

Hannah nodded and sprang into action to start up the computer, intent on candle-ordering the modern way.

Jenny began putting away pots that had dried in the rack, not troubling to hide a little smile of satisfaction. Hannah was here so often now, and she was eager to do so much. What a welcome change! She would have to start paying her a wage soon if this carried on.

'What are you going to call it?'

Jenny was startled out of her reverie.
'Pardon?'

'The shop. It has to have a name, doesn't it?'

'Oh, yes! You're right. I thought Good Times. What do you think?'

'Not bad. Better than Happy Times anyway!

'Oh?'

'You can't guarantee happiness, can you? But you can do something about goodness. Just stock good things.'

'Do you know, Hannah, I never would have thought of that. What a wonderful explanation. Thank you.'

Hannah ducked her head in acknowledgement.

She was pleased. Jenny smiled.

'What did he say?' Hannah asked a few moments later.

'Hm?'

'My dad. What did he say when you asked him?'

'Oh, he's too busy. He said he hasn't got the time.'

'He said what!'

Jenny turned to find Hannah staring fiercely at her.

'Is that really what he said?' Hannah demanded.

Jenny nodded.

'The lying, lazy, old has-been! He does nothing. Every day he does nothing at all. He just hangs about the house.'

'He looks after you and James,' Jenny said gently. 'You mustn't forget that. It can't be easy for him.'

'Looking after us?' Hannah said with a snort of derision. 'Thank you very much!'

'I mean since your mother passed away. It can't have been easy for him.'

'It hasn't been easy for me and James either. Anyway, she died. She didn't pass away.'

Hannah got up and headed for the door. Jenny listened to her feet clattering down the stairs. Oh, dear! she thought unhappily. What have I done now?

* * *

Will Renfrew had told her he lived in his grandfather's house, as had his parents before him. What he hadn't said was how grand it was. Tweed House was a very impressive property indeed.

'My goodness, Will! You didn't say you lived in a stately home'

'It's only a minor palace, this one, not one of Grandfather's better efforts. Come on in.'

It was a three-storey, stone-built house set in a large garden. Ancient sycamore trees guarded the perimeter. A gravelled drive led

50

up to the stone pillars supporting the porch over the front door. Ancient roses rambled and climbed over the south-facing wall, and they were flowering still, even in November, determined to make the best of what remained of the year, determined to put on a good show for a new visitor.

'Gosh, it's so posh! I feel as if I should have put on my best frock,' she said, allowing Will to lead her into the hall.

'You look very nice as you are,' he assured her. 'Far too good for Tweed House in fact.'

'Will, you say the nicest things!' She turned to admire the plaster work on the ceiling and the panelled walls.

'Like it?' Will asked with a smile.

'Very much.'

'A bit over-done for modern tastes, perhaps, but I like it too. I must do. I've never moved out, and I've not changed much of it.'

He took her through into a large room that was now the kitchen, but that she guessed from the ornamentation around the upper walls and ceiling hadn't always been where the cooking was done.

'You have altered things around a little, though?'

'Yes. The original kitchen was very cold and dark. So I converted this room into what the Americans call a kitchen-diner. This is where I live most of the time.'

Jenny nodded and turned around,

fascinated.

'It's a very big house, Will.'

'Too big for one person really. I'll show you the rest later. Now, would you like something to drink? Wine, tea, coffee?'

'Coffee would be good.'

'You'll stay for some lunch?'

'Oh . . . I hadn't thought . . . That's very nice of you, Will. Thank you. I'd like that.'

She'd come to see his work but now she was here she looked forward to seeing the rest of the house.

'Your grandfather must have been a very wealthy man?' she suggested.

'Yes, but I'm not,' Will said quickly, with a self-deprecating laugh. 'House rich, perhaps, but cash poor.'

'Oh, I didn't mean . . . I just meant how wonderful to have been able to design his own home, a house like this.'

Will poured the coffee before he responded. He did it carefully. She guessed he did most things carefully. It was his nature to look after things, to take care. The house was in good hands, but not, perhaps, enough of them.

'He was an interesting man from all accounts, my grandfather. Not that I ever knew him personally. But he must have been, from everything I know about him. He had two careers. In the first he was a ship owner, part of a syndicate, and he made a lot of money. In the second he was an architect and developer at the wrong time, and lost a lot of money. Pretty much all he had to leave when he died was this house.'

'What did your father do for a living?'

'He'd inherited the architecture gene. But he wasn't as ambitious or as good as his own father. So he made a comfortable living as an architect, but his practice was a local one. Porches, kitchen extensions, garages. That sort of thing.' He shrugged and added, 'It paid the bills. He and my mother had a very happy marriage, and a good life together.'

'And has the architecture gene been passed on again?'

'Alas, no!' He shook his head and said, 'Come on! Let me show you what I do.'

*   *   *

Will had a studio on the first floor. It was a big, cluttered room full of light from huge windows and colour from the vibrant acrylic landscapes that adorned almost every square inch of space on one wall.

Jenny shook her head in wonder. 'But these are gorgeous, Will!' she said, gazing with awe at a spectacular and enormous painting of sunset over the Cheviots. 'You must have been there at the time?'

He ducked his head in appreciation of the comment.

53

'At that very moment?' she pressed.

'I was. All night, in fact. Most of it, at least. It was mid-summer, when the darkness doesn't last long in this part of the country.'

She nodded and moved on, looking at other paintings in the collection. She liked what she saw. Landscapes were no longer fashionable in the galleries that displayed contemporary art, perhaps, but there would always be painters who would continue trying to do them justice. It was obvious that Will was one of them.

'Do they sell?' she asked.

'Some do.'

'Not enough?'

He shook his head. 'We struggle to make a living in our own lifetime, most of us painters. But in a hundred years' time there will probably be dealers and collectors making thousands out of these.'

She knew that was quite likely to be true. It seemed so unfair. 'But your portraits sell?'

'Oh, yes! Enough to allow me to hang on to this dilapidated old house, and to live in the style to which I am accustomed.'

She smiled. Will, again. He was always so modest and self-deprecating. Perhaps it was his way of warding off and coping with disappointment. Or perhaps he really was as happy and contented as he seemed. He had a good life, after all.

'I admire you, Will. I really do. You've

found a way of living the life you want, and doing the things important to you.'

He inclined his head again.

'And now,' he said, 'let me astonish you with my culinary skills. Lunch calls!'

Tom Offers A Helping Hand

'Has Harry Cummings been to see you yet?' Tom asked Jenny the next day.

She looked up, smiled and shook her head. 'Not yet, no. And to be honest, I don't expect him anytime soon!'

'But you still want the shop sorting out?'

'Of course I do, Tom! I need to make a living, and right now I can't even get started. I allowed myself a few weeks to get settled and sorted, but I'm running out of time now. And money.'

Tom looked thoughtful. She wondered if he'd come up with the name of another joiner for her. Someone who wasn't busy, which could only be because he wasn't a very good joiner. She didn't care. She wasn't proud. Not now. She needed somebody—anybody! Much more delay and she'd have to go and buy a hammer and saw, and try to do it herself!

'OK. I'll do it,' Tom said.

'What?'

'Refurbish the shop. I'll do the work for

55

you—if you still want me to, that is.'

The offer came as quite a shock. It wasn't at all what she'd been expecting. She wasn't sure how to respond. Was he serious?

'I thought you didn't have the time, Tom?'

'Aye, well.' He looked at her and shrugged. 'Hannah's persuaded me that I have. She says you're struggling. It helps that you live next door, of course—less travelling time.'

Jenny smiled with delight. 'You'd better come in, Tom. We can't discuss business out on the street'

'No, we don't want the neighbours to see us.'

'Tom! That's not what I meant at all,' she said, laughing.

*   *   *

She led him into the old shop and began telling him what she wanted done and invited his opinion on things she was unsure about.

'So,' he summarised after a little while, 'I'll replace the windows, strip the floor, put up shelves, a counter and display boxes.' He stopped and glanced round. 'What about the walls?'

She looked round at the crumbling, discoloured walls and tried not to shudder. 'A coat of paint, do you think?'

Tom shook his head. 'The plasterwork needs repairing.'

He stuck a finger into a crack and pulled a chunk of plaster loose, leaving a big bare patch behind.

'Oh, dear!' Jenny said, even more worried.

'It's nothing. I can fix that. Fill the gaps. Put a skim over it.'

'Really?'

He nodded. 'Best to do it before we start putting up shelves and decorating.'

Jenny was happy Tom was there, looking things over, suggesting solutions to problems. He seemed so different to his usual morose self.

'What?' he asked, seeing her looking at him.

'Nothing,' she said, giving him a smile. 'Just . . . Oh, I don't know! I'm just so happy you're here. That's all. It's so good to talk about all this to someone who knows what he's doing.'

What she didn't say was that it felt good to have him, Tom, there. She felt very comfortable in his presence these days. And, she admitted to herself, she found him a very attractive man.

She liked his black curly hair. She liked his eyes, and the way he studied things, looking at them carefully. Even more than that, she liked his presence, his strong, quiet presence. How wrong can you be? she wondered, thinking back to their difficult encounter the night she'd arrived in Cragley. What an unpleasant man he had seemed then.

57

She pulled herself together. Tom had moved on from studying the walls of the shop and was contemplating something else. He walked backwards and forwards a couple of times. Then he stamped on the floor in a few places.

She saw and felt the boards give slightly.

'I'll have a look under the floor while I'm at it,' he announced. 'The joists need some support. Maybe something's come loose, or broken away. Either that or there's a bit of rot or woodworm damage.'

Jenny's spirits began to sag again. It was beginning to look a bigger job than she had imagined.

'It's nothing,' Tom assured her. 'You're bound to get a bit of floor weakness after a hundred years of folk treading on the boards. It should be all right, basically. But it'll be best to sort it out before we do much else.'

Jenny nodded, her spirits recovering once again in the face of Tom's practical competence.

'Will there be a cellar you can get into?'

He shook his head. 'Just a big cavity if it's the same as mine—which it will be. I'll be able to get into it all right. There'll likely be a little entry somewhere that the electricians or the plumbers have made. I'll use that.'

He looked around again and added, 'That's about it.'

'It's enough! How long is it all going to

take?'

'A couple of weeks. Maybe less, if I get cracking.'

'Is that all?' Jenny was pleasantly surprised. 'Are you sure?'

'It's not a big job.'

'It seems it to me.'

He shook his head.

'What's it going to cost, do you think? Not that that matters much. The work has to be done.'

'I'll work out an estimate for you, but I'm not expensive. I'm cheaper than Harry Cummings, anyway,' he added with a mischievous smile. 'He'd want to make it seaworthy!'

She laughed and invited him into the kitchen for a cup of tea.

What a wonderful start to the day! she thought. The prospect of progress at last.

'Hannah says you've been buying stock for the shop,' Tom said. 'What have you been doing with it?'

'I thought I'd better keep the shop clear until the work was done. So I've been putting it in the big shed at the bottom of the garden.'

'Good idea.'

'It's a good shed, actually. I was surprised. It's more of a workshop than a storage shed.'

Tom nodded. 'Craig Dalglish set it up. He used to live here, years ago. He was a bit of a craftsman himself. Wood turner. Just amateur,

59

mind, but he turned out some good stuff. I had my eye on his workshop myself at one time.'

'What happened?'

'It's a long story.'

He shuffled and began to get to his feet.

Jenny wondered what the story could be, but accepted that it was off-limits. Probably a plan he and his wife had had in mind. She didn't ask.

'By the way, Tom, Hannah has been wonderful. She's been helping me such a lot lately. You'd be amazed at what she's done.'

He looked a bit uncertain, puzzled even. She told him what they'd been up to, planning what to stock and ordering online for the shop.

'I thought something must have changed in that girl's life,' he admitted, 'but I didn't know the half of it.'

'Didn't she tell you?'

'She said she'd been here once or twice, but not what she'd been doing. I'm amazed!'

'Young people, eh? They don't get enough credit.'

'Thank you for spending time with her, Jenny. Not everyone would. I'm grateful.'

'Not at all, Tom. I like her. Besides, she's been an enormous help. In fact, I'm thinking of offering her a little wage to continue helping me. If you wouldn't object?'

'She'd like that!' He chuckled. 'Thanks

again. She's been a worry to me since Annie died. I mean, she's getting older now, and coming to a time in her life when a father can't give her everything she needs. Advice, and so on,' he added awkwardly. 'Women's concerns.'

'I understand. But you're doing fine, Tom. So is Hannah. You don't need to worry about her.'

He nodded. 'I just wish I could say the same about the other one,' he added darkly.

'James?'

'Yes, James.'

'Oh dear. You sound fed-up. What's the problem there?'

Tom sighed and looked close to despair. 'He's got a date with the magistrates coming up.'

'For not attending school? Surely not?'

'For vandalism, they say, and persistent trouble-making.'

Jenny thought quickly. 'He's not been in trouble before, has he?'

'Only every day!'

She grimaced. 'I'm sorry, Tom. I hope things work out for him, and for you.'

'Aye,' Tom said miserably. 'So do I.'

A Smile From James

'Is something wrong, Hannah?' asked Jenny, concerned, watching the girl as she worked.

'No. Where do you want these soaps putting?'

'Those hand-made, sweet-scented, pastel-shaded, carefully-wrapped tablets of bath-time delight?'

'Yeah, those.'

'In the shed, please.'

Hannah went off willingly enough but Jenny was worried about her. She wasn't her usual self. Her sense of humour had deserted her, for one thing. She was too quiet, for another. But Jenny didn't want to press her. Not yet. She didn't want to add to whatever pressures the girl was already experiencing.

She made a mug of coffee for herself and got out a carton of fruit juice for Hannah. Then she began making some scones. How domesticated I've become, she thought with a wry smile.

'Sit down, Hannah!' she ordered when the girl returned. 'Have a rest. You deserve it. And help yourself to juice.' Hannah sat down and slumped in a disconsolate heap.

Jenny took pity on her and stopped what she was doing. She rinsed the flour from her fingers and dried her hands.

'Hannah?' she said quietly, and was appalled by the tearful face that was turned towards her. 'What is it, dear? What . . .'

'It's James!'

'James? I don't understand.'

'He's been at it again—and he blames me! I know he does.'

'What's he done now?'

'He's been fighting on the school bus. Him and Greg McCord.'

It was news to Jenny that James had even been on the school bus. Good news, actually.

'Oh! Has he been going to school?'

Jenny shook her head. 'Sometimes he goes on the bus, though.'

'Whatever for?'

'He spends the day in Berwick. A few of them do that. I do it sometimes,' she added defiantly.

Jenny took that in her stride. The situation was complicated enough.

'So why does he blame you?'

'He thinks I should have been there with him. Then it wouldn't have happened. That's what twins are for, he says to stick together.'

'What does your dad say?'

Hannah sniffed. 'Not much. He says he's going to find work for James to do, to keep him out of mischief. But he's worried as well. I know he is. He doesn't want the police coming to the door.'

'He won't want to see James in any more

63

trouble either,' Jenny suggested.

'No.'

'Maybe he could come and help us?'

'In the shop? I don't think so.'

'No. We don't have a lot of scope for fighting in here.

A faint smile crept across Hannah's face. Jenny decided it was a good sign.

'What does James like doing? Playing football?'

Hannah shook her head.

'What, then?'

'He's really into computers. I don't mean just playing games and stuff. He likes messing about with their workings.'

'You've got one at home?'

'An old one.'

'What does he do? Apart from play games on it?'

'He likes taking it to bits and putting it back together again.' She grinned and added, 'Dad doesn't know he does that. He'd probably go mad if he did!'

'I'll bet,' Jenny said thoughtfully.

*   *   *

Jenny was impressed with the way Tom set to work. He hadn't been in the house five minutes when the sounds of hammering and sawing began. Soon she could smell the unfamiliar scent of sawdust in the air. She

64

hurried to shut doors before it got everywhere. He seemed to know what he was doing, though, she thought with satisfaction. And progress was being made in the shop. At last!

When she went out to go to the village store, she was astonished to see her old windows were already removed and lying outside on the footpath. Even more astonishing was the sight of James wielding a hammer as if he meant business.

'Hello, James! I didn't know you were here, as well.'

'I have to be, don't I?' came the sullen reply.

'He's helping me,' Tom said sharply, putting an end to it.

Jenny couldn't help smiling to herself as she went on her way. Maybe the boy was protesting too much. There was an energy and commitment about the pair of them that was unexpected. Maybe they'd both needed something to do, she thought happily. But, then, don't we all?

*   *   *

Later, she had an idea. She waited until Tom was out of the way, on an errand to Berwick for some special screws and other things he was short of, and then she approached James, who was collecting together scrap wood and

65

sweeping up.

'How's it going?'

'All right.'

He didn't look round or stop sweeping.

'You've got the new windows in, I see?'

'Yeah.'

It was like getting blood from a stone but she persisted. 'James, Hannah tells me you're interested in computers?' He gave her a quick, suspicious look but said nothing.

'I've got an old one I want rid of. Would it be of any use to you?'

'What sort is it?'

She told him. He was non-committal. He really was hard work, she thought. She pitied the teachers at his school. 'Maybe you could cannibalise it use it for spare parts?'

'It's a newer one than ours,' he said reluctantly.

'Is it? So you might be able to use it?'

'Maybe. I'll have to take a look. How much do you want for it?'

'Nothing. If you don't want it, I'll just have to see if the council will collect it and take it away.'

'Let's have a look now, then,' James said, coming to a decision, 'before our dad gets back.'

The computer was fine, actually. It was in working order. Nothing wrong with it. But she'd bought a new one with more capacity, just before the move. She'd known she would be doing a lot of research and ordering online. So it had seemed a sensible investment. But she hadn't been able to bring herself to throw the old one away. It was a good thing she hadn't, she thought now with relief.

'I'll take it off your hands,' James said gravely, once he'd taken a look. 'If you're sure?'

'Oh, yes,' she assured him. 'Please take it.'

To her surprise, James smiled and said, 'Thanks.'

Lunch With Tom

Suddenly Tom had finished work and the shop was ready. Empty but ready. 'All yours now,' he told Jenny with a smile. 'You can fill it with whatever you want. I've done my bit.'

He'd done an excellent job. She saw that at once. The re-plastered and fresh-painted walls. The new windows. The stripped floorboards. The shelves and display units, and the counter top. He'd even had someone he knew come in to install new wiring and lighting, placing downlighters and spotlights exactly where she wanted them.

'It's wonderful, Tom!' she breathed excitedly. 'I can't thank you enough.'

She turned and beamed at him.

He shrugged and gazed around

nonchalantly. 'It's not bad, is it?'

'Not bad? It's terrific!'

She forgot herself and gave him a little hug, she was so excited.

'Sorry,' she said, seeing him flinch, realising she had embarrassed him.

He laughed, recovering. 'Nothing to be sorry about,' he said. 'I just wish all my clients were so appreciative. Generally, I just get complaints.'

'I'm sure that's not true.'

She broke away to investigate the shop that he had created. In her mind's eye she was plotting where things would go. Hand-made candles here. The wooden toys against the back wall. Maybe some of them could even hang from the ceiling? The downlighters would show off the jewellery beautifully in the case she'd had made. Oh, it would be wonderful! But so much to consider—and to do.

What about the hand-made paper items Hannah had spotted and ordered? Where would they go? She grimaced. Store them in the shed at first, probably. No point trying to cram too much in here. But she'd better ask Hannah first.

'Where's Hannah?' she asked, turning back to Tom. 'What?' she demanded, seeing the big grin on his face.

He shook his head. 'Nothing,' he said. 'I was just enjoying watching you being carried away.'

'Oh, Tom! You have no idea. It's wonderful. Finally, at last, after two whole years of planning and thinking and worrying, I can set up shop. You've no idea what it means to me.'

'I'm happy for you,' he said, nodding with understanding. 'By the way, is it still to be called Good Times?'

'Yes, it is,' she said, surprised he knew.

'Hannah told me. It's a good name.'

'Thank you.'

'If you're sticking to that, I know a man who paints shop fronts and does fancy signs. I can get him to call in and talk to you about it, if you like?'

'Oh, excellent! I was wondering what to do about that.' She took a deep breath and beamed with pleasure. 'Thank you so much for what you've done here, Tom. We're just about there now. And you've helped make my dream come true.'

'Aye, well.' He was fidgeting now, uncomfortable with her emotional words. 'I'll be getting on. Hannah's gone over to see her friend at High Town Farm, by the way. She'll not be back till this evening.'

'Oh, yes. I forgot. She did tell me. Where are you going?' she demanded, seeing him edge towards the door.

'Got to get on. Things to do,' he muttered vaguely.

'Not yet, you haven't!' She smiled and beckoned to him. 'This calls for a celebration. Come on! I'll buy you lunch at The Leaping Salmon.'

'You'll buy me lunch?'

'Definitely.'

'I don't know if that would be right.'

'Well, I do. I owe you such a lot. Besides, there's more business to talk about.'

'Oh?'

'So fetch your coat. Let's go. I'm starving.'

He looked at her speculatively for a long moment. Then he smiled the smile that she was beginning to associate with him. He wasn't scowling nearly so much these days.

*   *   *

The pub was as busy as it had been the last time she was there. Even more so, she thought, gazing round with interest. 'It's a popular place, isn't it?'

He nodded. 'They do a good meal here.'

She wondered how he knew. Eating out? Old times, probably. They ordered. Then it was time to talk business.

'Tom, you've done a super job on the shop. You really have.'

He chuckled. 'Surprised you, eh?'

'Well . . .'

'I liked the work, actually. I enjoyed it. Once I got started, I realised how much I'd

70

missed it.'

'In that case, maybe you should keep it up?'

'How do you mean?'

'Well, if my experience is anything to go by, Cragley doesn't have enough working joiners and carpenters. I could have been waiting until next year for Harry Cummings to turn up.'

'Or the year after, maybe.'

'Or the one after that. If then—if ever!'

'There's certainly plenty of work for a skilled man,' Tom said cautiously. 'I'll give you that. And I could do with the money.'

'Well, then?'

He looked at her suspiciously. 'Well then, what?'

'Announce that you're available—open for business—and get your life back on track. Why not?'

'It's not easy, though, is it?' he said, looking uncertain now.

'It could be, Tom. What's the problem?'

He looked as if he was wrestling with a huge weight. Her heart went out to him.

'I'll go up to the bar and order coffee for us,' he told her, changing the subject.

Jenny watched him go. She guessed that the reason for his reluctance to get back to work wasn't to do with the twins, who were old enough now to look after themselves. It was more to do with a lack of confidence. That could have such a debilitating effect.

71

She'd heard it said, or she'd read somewhere, that if you were unemployed for a year you were officially classified as 'long-term unemployed', a notoriously difficult group to be in.

And if you were out of work longer then that, then the chances were you would never work again.

Tom returned with two coffees and a big grin. 'Hilda's run off her feet,' he said, referring to the waitress. 'She said if I brought the coffees over myself, we could have them for free.'

'And you managed all by yourself?'

Still grinning, he set the cups down. 'Some things I can do,' he said.

'There are a lot of things you can do,' she told him gently. But she didn't want to press him. Not today. Not after everything he had done for her.

'What are you thinking?' he said, catching her looking at him.

'Nothing.'

'What are you thinking?' he insisted.

'Oh, I was just thinking how smart and handsome you look today. I've got used to seeing you covered in sawdust and plaster. There's not even any paint on that sweater.'

'I scrub up quite well, don't I?' he said, carefully dusting imaginary bits of fluff off his jumper, which was navy-blue and nice and chunky. Just right for the season.

'That colour suits you,' she added.

'Think so? The kids bought me this last Christmas.'

'Oh? It's nice. It looks a good one.'

'It's not cashmere.'

'No?'

'No imported rubbish like that. This is genuine Shetland wool.'

She laughed at his fierce expression. 'Cashmere isn't rubbish, actually. Though I agree, you're definitely more of a Shetland wool sort of man. I bet you have a genuine Harris Tweed jacket, as well, don't you?'

'Somewhere. In the wardrobe, I expect.' He looked at her with a twinkle and added, 'Are you trying to take the mickey?'

'Who, me?' she said, rolling her eyes. 'Would I ever?'

He grinned.

This was better, she thought happily. They were more comfortable with each other now, more so than they had ever been. Little things. Teasing. Being relaxed. What a difference they made.

'I can't abide sarcastic women,' he said now with mock severity. 'They make me forget I'm a gentleman.'

'I'll remember that,' she assured him.

He grinned again and stretched lazily. 'Muscles stiff?'

He nodded. 'They'd forgotten what work is like.'

73

She smiled. 'You've really pushed yourself hard this last couple of weeks. I know that.'

'Just a bit,' he agreed.

Then she found herself thinking how handsome he was when he was relaxed. And how much more at ease with himself he seemed now he'd finished the job. He was right. The work had been good for him.

Well, we all need a sense of purpose, she thought. Every one of us. Mum had given her one for so long. Now it was the shop. Tom had the twins, of course. But he'd needed more than that. He still did.

'This is the life!' Tom said now, spreading himself, smiling. 'Wining and dining. I could live like this.'

'Couldn't we all?'

'I was thinking,' he added a moment later. 'About what you said.'

She waited.

'Maybe I ought to pick up the tools again.'

'You already have,' she pointed out gently.

'But there's the kids still to be watched over.'

'Hannah's not a problem.'

'No, she isn't. Not now. She's even going to school again. Some days.'

'I did wonder about that'

He looked at her and added, 'I have you to thank for that. I know now what's been going on. You've done a lot for her.'

'She's a good girl, Tom. And very capable. I

like her a lot.'

He nodded.

'In fact, I'm hoping she'll continue to help me with the shop in her spare time.'

'I'm sure she will.'

'If she leaves school in the summer I might be able to keep her on and pay her a proper wage, depending on how business is.'

'She might stop on at school.'

'What makes you think that?'

'She's hinted at it.'

'That would be wonderful! So much better for her to get some qualifications.'

Tom nodded.

'Well, if she does, she can still help me part-time if she wants to. It will be up to her. So Hannah's not a problem. You don't need to be home all the time for her now.'

Tom looked cheerful for a moment. Then he scowled. 'James,' he said. 'He's the problem.'

Jenny thought that was probably true. She also thought it a good idea to by-pass the problem of James for a moment, and stay positive. Better to get back to Tom himself.

'If you start getting work, Tom, you'll need a workshop, won't you?'

'Aye.'

'I've been thinking about that. Would my shed be suitable?'

He looked up. 'How do you mean?'

'I really don't need such a big place for

75

storage. You'd be welcome to use it, if it's suitable.'

'That's very good of you, Jenny. Your shed would make a grand workshop. I'd pay you rent, of course.'

'Of course,' she agreed, though she hadn't thought of that at all, and didn't want to think of it. She just wanted to help.

'You do so much to help us,' Tom said wonderingly.

'And you and the twins do so much to help me,' she replied, realising with surprise how much she meant it. 'It's like being part of the family I've never had.'

*   *   *

Back at the house, after she and Tom had gone their separate ways, she was surprised to find James hanging around, waiting for her. She saw him before he saw her, and wondered what problem he was bringing with him. His gloom was palpable as he hung around outside her front door, hands deep in pockets.

'James! Are you waiting for me?'

Astonishingly, his face lit up in a smile. 'Not really,' he said. Then he added, 'I just wanted to say the computer's pretty good. It's a lot better than our old one.'

'I'm just glad it's found a good home.'

He nodded. Then his face turned serious again and he added, 'Hannah says you're having problems with your new one? Too slow, she says.'

'It is a bit, yes. It's all right, though. Just slow. Hannah says it's nothing like as fast as the ones at your school.'

'I could take a look at it, if you like? See if I can speed it up a bit. Sometimes they get clogged up with unnecessary programmes that you'll never need.'

She hesitated only a moment. 'Why, thank you, James! I'd appreciate it if you would.'

As she led the way inside, it was all Jenny could do to avoid shaking her head with amazement.

The Grand Opening

'For me?' Jenny said with surprise. The delivery man checked the label again. 'One dozen red roses,' he intoned. 'Jenny Morrison, Providence Lane, Cragley.'

'Well, the name and address are correct.'

'You've got an admirer,' the delivery man said with a knowing smile. 'Sign here, please.'

She signed and thanked him. Then she turned to take the box of flowers into the house, still puzzled.

'What have you got there?' Hannah asked.

'Oh . . . I'm not sure,' she said, laying the box on the bench.

77

'It looks like flowers,' Hannah said, scanning the label on the box. *'Flowers from Jersey* it says.'

'Yes,' Jenny admitted. 'I don't know who's sent them, though.'

Hannah grinned. 'A mystery man!' she said.

'Perhaps,' Jenny agreed with a puzzled smile. 'Now, how are you getting on with that order?'

There was so much to do now that the shop fitting was complete and Jenny soon realised she had seriously underestimated the preparation needed.

It wasn't just a case of sorting out the displays and thinking about pricing, although that did take time. It was also the ordering of candles and soaps, pottery and toys, ornaments and jewellery, and then the checking of the orders, and the chasing up of things that had been promised but hadn't arrived.

Then there were invoices and cheques to be dealt with. As well as sorting out everything with the bank in Berwick, and trying to find out from the tax man what were legitimate expenses that could be offset against her income.

Add to that the need to arrange for business cards and promotional leaflets to be printed, contacting local craftspeople and other potential suppliers. And . . . Oh, thousands of things!

Fortunately, she had Hannah's help some of the time. The girl was wonderful. So involved, so quick and eager to learn and be a part of it all. And so skilled, surprisingly. 'You're very good on the computer,' Jenny said, watching Hannah's fingers fly over the keyboard.

'Not really. Just simple stuff. You should see our James.'

'I don't need to see James. I can see you!' Hannah flashed her a grin. 'I'm your right-hand man, eh?'

'You are indeed.'

It was true. The shop would have been a lot further away from opening day without Hannah's assistance.

Jenny wondered sometimes about the summer, and what Hannah would be doing then. If she did leave school, could she afford to offer her full-time employment? She had no idea. Probably not, though, which would be a shame.

But would full-time employment in a gift shop serve Hannah well? Wouldn't it be better to encourage her to look further afield? Maybe. She was so young, though. Too young to be encouraged to move to a town, still less a city, in pursuit of a career. It really would be best if she stayed on at school.

But Jenny would, she decided, cross that bridge when she came to it. For now, she had enough to think about. Including who might have sent her a dozen red roses. That was something to ponder. Such intrigue!

She couldn't believe any of her friends back in Dartford were responsible. Yet she knew so few people here. Who did she know? Will? She smiled and chuckled. Of course! It was just the sort of gallant, old-fashioned thing he would do.

*   *   *

Came the day when they had done everything that could possibly be done to prepare the shop for opening. 'That's it,' said Tom. 'You'll be able to open tomorrow. You're all ready now.'

'But I'm not, am I?' Jenny said, worry eating away at her. 'We're short of all sorts of things.'

'What you haven't got,' Tom said firmly, 'you can do without.'

'What are we still missing, Hannah? Remind me.'

Hannah sprang to it, her young mind a veritable memory bank. 'The model soldiers haven't arrived yet. We're still waiting for the healing crystals. That woman from Country Preserves hasn't brought us her marmalade yet.'

Jenny looked at Tom and raised her eyebrows. There you are, then! she mimed.

Tom shrugged. 'You'll never miss them,' he

said firmly.

'That's about it,' Hannah said. 'Apart from the fact that James still has something to do on the computer. And the man from the council wants to talk to you about Council Tax, or something.'

Jenny nodded and did another mental review. 'The coffee?' she said to Hannah. 'Has that come?'

Hannah shook her head. 'Not that special flavoured coffee you ordered, but there's plenty of the ordinary left. That will do for them, won't it?'

The customers, she meant. Jenny frowned. She'd wanted the hazelnut-flavoured coffee. Something special for opening day.

'You've done everything you can,' Tom said. 'Get an early night. You've got a big day tomorrow.'

He was right. She knew that. If she didn't stop herself now, she would be fiddling about with things all night long.

'You're right,' she said, turning to him with a big smile. 'Enough's enough.'

Hannah got up from her chair and collected her coat and bag. She grinned at Jenny. 'It's going to be great, tomorrow, isn't it? I can't wait!'

'It is,' Jenny agreed. 'It's going to be lovely.'

She smiled and added, 'And I can't thank you both enough—and James—for helping me get to this point. You've been wonderful.

All of you.'

Hannah gave her a hug. Tom looked as if he wanted to. Then they were gone. She was left to her own devices.

*   *   *

It should have been a difficult, nervy time for her. But it wasn't. She had decided there was nothing more she could do tonight, and so she was able to relax. She needed to. Tomorrow was going to be a demanding day.

She wondered what Mum would have thought. The same as her, probably. She would have been excited and nervous, just as she was herself. Proud, too, probably. She was that herself, or she would be once tomorrow was over.

No! she told herself sternly. Stop that. Just to have got this far was something to be proud of. With the help of Hannah and Tom, she had converted dreams into reality. Even James had done something useful. She was almost satisfied.

*   *   *

The next morning started off well. Hannah arrived before Jenny had even had any breakfast. The sun was shining. There was no wind or rain. The shop looked quietly ready and eager for customers.

82

'I must get something to eat before we open,' Jenny said to Hannah, as she let her inside. 'Will you join me?'

'Had mine,' Hannah said. 'I was up early.'

'Well, come and talk to me while I have some breakfast.'

She didn't want much. She never did have much. Just her usual.

'I like apple juice,' Hannah said, watching Jenny pour a glass of orange juice. 'And coffee.'

Jenny's pot of tea was ready. 'So you don't want any of this?'

Hannah shook her head.

'You can make yourself some coffee, if you like. What about muesli? Do you like that for breakfast?'

'Nuts and stuff?' Hannah shook her head and wrinkled her nose. 'Not much.'

'Would you like to try some?'

'Just a bit then.'

Jenny smiled to herself as she served up orange juice, muesli and tea, and watched Hannah overcome her declared preferences.

'What have we got to do this morning?' Hannah asked. 'Put on the coffee machine? Open the door? Wait?'

Hannah grinned. 'I can do all that!'

'And a lot more besides, young lady. I'd never have got to this point without you'

A full minute went by. Then Hannah leapt to her feet. 'Maybe I should open the door

83

now?'

'Goodness, Hannah! You're a slave driver. I don't intend opening the shop as early as this. It's only half-past eight.'

Then she relented as Hannah sat back down. 'Go on, then! Go and do it. Just this once we can open early.'

Hannah needed no second invitation. She was away down the stairs instantly.

Jenny smiled and shook her head. She had been trying to pace herself and not get caught up in a mad frenzy. Not that she expected many customers on the first morning. Not for a shop like hers, in a place like Cragley. That would be expecting far too much.

When she went downstairs, she found Hannah already had the OPEN sign on the shop door and the coffee machine gurgling. They exchanged smiles.

We're ready, Jenny thought. At last!

*   *   *

Soon afterwards the door bell jangled. They both looked round.

'It's only me!' Wendy from the village shop was standing in the doorway. 'I just called to wish you luck. I hope you have a really good day. You deserve it.'

'Thank you, Wendy! That's sweet of you. Will you have a cup of coffee with us?'

'I haven't got time. I have to open my own

shop in ten minutes.'

'A small cup?'

'Oh, go on, then!'

Wendy came inside and stood looking around. 'My! You have got it nice. It looks lovely. So much stock, as well. Where's it all come from?'

'It's a start,' Jenny acknowledged, pleased by her reaction.

'And I see you have a helper.'

'Oh, yes. I couldn't have managed without Hannah. I can't now either. We're a team.'

Hannah grinned.

'Well, good for you both! And what about James?' Wendy added. 'Has he been helping, as well?'

'Sometimes,' Hannah said quickly. 'But he's got a lot on at the minute. He helps my dad a lot.'

Wendy nodded gravely. 'Young people, eh?' she said, giving Jenny a slow wink. 'What a help they can be.'

Jenny hid a smile and nodded. Wendy probably didn't realise how right she was.

*   *   *

Soon after Wendy left, the same man who'd delivered the mysterious red roses arrived. This time he handed Jenny a beautiful bouquet containing more flowers than she had ever seen before in one cellophane packet.

85

'For me?' she gasped.

'Seems to be.' The man smiled and added, 'You've got a really big admirer!'

Jenny smiled back, and peered at the note May All Your Times Be Good Times, she read out aloud. 'That's lovely!' she said with delight.

By the time she'd signed the receipt and seen the delivery man to the door, Hannah had brought a big vase of water. 'Thank you, Hannah. Aren't they lovely?'

The girl nodded and smiled happily.

'But who sent them, I wonder?'

Hannah shook her head, still smiling.

Will again, probably. It had to be. She must remember to thank him.

'Oh, what a wonderful day, Hannah. What a wonderful day!

She grasped a laughing Hannah, and they performed an impromptu waltz around the shop.

*   *   *

The first real customer was Mrs Jackson from the village, looking for a gift for one of her many, many grandchildren, or great-grandchildren—she was no longer very sure.

'You've got it very nice,' she said, gazing round with fascination. 'It's much better now than when Tommy Mavin had it.'

'Tommy Mavin?' Jenny queried.

'The butcher.'

Hannah giggled.

'Goodness! I'm glad to hear I've improved on his efforts! That must have been a long time ago.'

'Oh, it was. I was only little then. But I haven't been in here since. We didn't get on, you know. His family and mine.'

Jenny smiled and wondered what year it could have been when Mrs Jackson was last in the shop. Probably when the Queen was still called Victoria.

The old lady eventually bought a wooden toy with moving parts—a clown on a bicycle. And that was their first sale.

Other customers came after her. They came in a slow trickle, usually in ones but occasionally in twos. Some bought. Some just looked round. All were pleasant and eager to talk. Jenny relaxed. Hannah grew bored. The morning passed. Good Times was truly in business. In good time for Christmas, as well.

House Guests

Jenny couldn't wait to see them. Lucy and Kate were her two best friends from Dartford. Until the phone call from Lucy, she hadn't realised how much she'd missed them.

'If you could find it in your heart to

87

welcome two old friends who are positively
aching to see you again and who are dying to
get a look at your Northern wilderness . . . If
you have the slightest, tiniest little bit of spare
room . . .'
'Oh, Luce! Stop it. Stop it at once!' Jenny
was laughing herself silly. 'You know I would
love it if you could manage a visit.'
'Really?'
'When do you think you might be able to
come?'
'As soon as we can both manage it! I'll tell
Kate right now.'

*   *   *

The visit was arranged for a couple of weeks
ahead, in early December, when the girls'
respective husbands were to be somewhere in
Spain playing golf. Lucy also had two children,
but kindly grandparents had arranged to look
after them and take them on a visit to an
outdoor leisure centre that the children had
been to before and loved.
'I should tell you, though,' Jenny warned,
'that I've got the shop open now.'
'Already? How wonderful! What's it like?
No, don't tell me. Let it be a surprise.'
'I'll just say that it's very nice. I'm pleased
with it.'
Lucy had second thoughts. 'Oh, but you
won't want us there now, will you? You must

be far too busy. We'd just get in the way.
We . . .'
'Come, Luce! Come whenever you can.'
'Are you sure?'
'Yes.'
'Oh, good! We can help. We can sell things.
Well, maybe I'll struggle a bit, but I'm sure
Kate won't. Kate would be brilliant in a shop.
I've always thought so. She's . . .'
Jenny stopped listening. Lucy was famous
for her non-stop prattle, as well as for her
generosity and good nature. Even if she
couldn't sell anything, she would be a
wonderful asset in the shop. People would
come from miles around just to experience
her.
For a while, Jenny forgot how busy she was.
She simply couldn't wait to see Kate and Lucy.

*   *   *

Now the day of their arrival was here and
Jenny had driven into Berwick to meet the
girls from the London train. She was shivering
with anticipation. Scarcely able to conceal her
excitement. It had been three months since
she'd seen anyone from her old life. Longer.
Four. Now she was about to see the two
people she'd missed most of all.
    If they hadn't forgotten, or changed their
minds. And if the train hadn't broken down,
or the tracks weren't being repaired,

maintained, upgraded, or whatever else they could do to two steel rails if people in high places set their minds to it.

But here it was at last. The train!

She watched the gleaming, silvery tube glide effortlessly alongside the platform until it slowed down and shivered to a stop with a last sigh, already most of the way from King's Cross to Edinburgh.

Jenny waited anxiously, half-full of excitement, half-full of dread that for some reason they wouldn't be on the train after all

But they were. She spotted Kate's flounce of red hair first as she hurtled out of the door, followed by a dignified blonde lady swaddled in numerous scarves and an enormous coat that hung down nearly to her ankles. Jenny gasped and shook her head. Then she grinned and rushed to meet them.

They spotted her. Lucy squealed. Kate rushed at her. They met and formed a small circle, and hugged one another, oblivious to the people rushing past.

'It's so good to see you!' Jenny gasped. 'Thank you so much for coming.'

'So you have missed us?' Kate said, laughing and stepping back.

'Oh, yes!'

'We did wonder, didn't we, Luce?'

'We did indeed, but I said she wouldn't have forgotten us altogether.'

'Oh, Luce!' Jenny gazed happily at Lucy.

'What on earth have you got on?' she asked, laughing and stroking the impressive coat.

'It's my new winter coat. You need a winter coat if you're coming to this part of the world.'

'Luce, it's a lovely day here!'

It was, too. Mild and sunny with hardly any wind.

'I did tell her,' Kate said. 'I said it wasn't the North Pole —quite!'

'I'm so hot,' Lucy complained, starting to unfasten her coat. 'It was hot in the train, and it's hot here. Why did nobody tell me?'

'I did!' Kate said. 'I did tell you.'

'But not firmly enough. Not clearly. You just said it might not be so very cold. What on earth does that mean?'

Jenny, still laughing, seized both her friends by the arm and started to move them along the platform, heading for the exit.

'You're blonde now?' she pointed out, looking at Lucy's flowing locks.

'Blondes have more fun, Jenny. Didn't anyone tell you?'

'I'd forgotten that.'

'It's not true, anyway,' Kate said. 'She has a lot less fun than me.'

'That's not true!' Lucy wailed. Then she looked around. 'Is this Scotland?' she demanded. 'If it is, why are the men all wearing trousers instead of kilts? I do love men in kilts.'

'It's not quite Scotland,' Jenny said,

91

laughing. 'Some say it is, of course, and probably it was once. But legally, Berwick-upon-Tweed is still in England. Come on! Let's go.'

She piled them into the car and got moving. But it was hard to concentrate on her driving. There were so many questions. They all had them, and they all asked them. Lucy also had her inevitable running commentary on everything they passed and saw, and even the things they didn't see.

'No highland pipe band to welcome us, Jen?' Kate asked. 'Later,' Jenny told her. 'Be patient.'

As they neared Cragley, Jenny felt proud as she anticipated showing her old friends around her new home.

'How quiet it is here,' Kate marvelled. 'No traffic at all. Is it always like this?'

'Most of the time.'

'Hm,' Lucy said. 'But there must be bright lights somewhere?'

'Not a one,' Jenny told her. 'You're just going to have to do without them for a few days.'

'I suppose I could re-charge my batteries while I'm here. Is that what you've been doing all this time?'

'Me? I've been very busy; very busy indeed. Here we are.' She pulled into the side of the road.

'This it?' Kate said, gazing out of the

window.

'This is it!'

'My, oh my!'

'It looks a big place,' Lucy ventured. 'And the shop! Oh, I can't wait to see it.'

*   *   *

'It's a lovely old house, Jen,' Kate said, after having been shown around. 'It's gorgeous.'

'Thank you. I'm glad you like it.'

'It's great that all the period detail remains —the fireplaces, the plasterwork, and so on. And I love the staircase. All those spindles! It's like a staircase in an illustration from an old-fashioned children's book.'

'I know just what you mean!' Jenny nodded vigorously. 'There should be a coat stand in the hall, with a place for umbrellas.'

'And a cupboard under the stairs where small people can hide and hear delicious grown-up secrets.'

Exactly, thought Jenny, laughing hard.

'Luce?' Kate said. 'You're unusually quiet. No opinions?'

Lucy swung round in a slow pirouette. 'I'm just thinking what a great place this would be to have a party!'

'Oh, Luce!' Kate said. 'Don't you ever stop?'

'It is a lovely house, though,' Lucy said. 'I quite agree. You've done ever so well, Jen.

93

And the shop's gorgeous. I bet you couldn't have afforded a place like this back home.'

'Certainly not on my salary at the bank.' Jenny smiled. 'That, of course, was one reason I moved north.'

'And you don't find the climate too . . . too chilly?'

'Oh, Luce! Of course not. It is the same country, you know. Millions of people live even further north than this.'

'Yes, but they're Scots. They're hardy people. Not like you and I, or even Kate.'

'Don't be so silly! Anyway, you've seen what the weather's like today. It's not that unusual.'

'What about the natives?' Lucy persisted. 'The Northumbrians? Are they friendly?'

'Friends and neighbours,' Jenny said firmly. 'In this village that's what we call them. Natives indeed!'

'Friends and neighbours? How quaint. Will we get to meet any?'

'They'll be hard to avoid. I've made a few friends. Wendy in the village shop. Tom next door, and his children. And Will Renfrew.'

'Tom, Will . . . ? You have been busy.'

She looked at Kate meaningfully.

'I think Jenny must be having a lovely time,' Kate said tactfully.

'Yes?' Lucy said, narrowing her eyes thoughtfully at Jenny. 'I bet she is. No wonder she's happy here.'

'Tea anyone?' Jenny said brightly. 'Coffee?'

Friendly Advice

'Ladies!' Will said, doffing an imaginary hat. 'How was your journey?'

'It took absolutely ages,' Lucy told him in her best posh voice. 'Hours!'

'Four,' Kate added.

Will shook his head in apparent amazement. Then he turned to Jenny. 'Such good friends you have, my dear. Travelling all this way, enduring such a journey, just to see you. Not that it wasn't worth it, I might add! I would be the first to do just the same, given the opportunity.'

'Oh, shut up, Will! You're worse than Lucy.'

Jenny wasn't sure if she was amused or indignant. Lucy was up to her old tricks again —playing up to men. And Will responding to the challenge like some Edwardian admirer.

'Let me introduce you to my old friends, Kate and Lucy,' she said hastily. 'And this is Will Renfrew he's an artist,' she added tartly.

'Artist?' Lucy said in her most breathless voice. 'Oh, how wonderful!'

Not to be outdone, Kate smiled and said, 'I've long wanted to meet a real artist, Will. All I ever seem to meet in Dartford are people who paint pictures of dogs and cats, and babies and things!'

'Ah!' Will smiled, nodded with

understanding and looked towards Jenny. 'I'll just make a pot of tea,' Jenny announced with a wicked smile. 'I'll leave you three to get better acquainted.'

* * *

Will stayed for an hour, chatting and laughing with Jenny and her friends, then he left to get back to his latest commission. But never one to conceal her thoughts for long, Lucy again took up the subject of Jenny's artistic neighbour at the earliest opportunity. 'Are you interested in him, Jen? Seriously interested?'

Jenny smiled. 'Of course I am. He's a good friend. He's a very nice man. Anyone would find him interesting.'

Lucy waved a hand impatiently. 'Of course they would. But that's not the point, is it?'

'She means interested romantically,' Kate added helpfully. 'As in seeing him. Going out with him. Having designs on him. But you don't need to answer that question. If you don't want to, that is.'

'Of course she needs to answer it!' Lucy protested. 'I didn't come all this way to have Jenny introduce me to this adorable man—who paints wonderful portraits of dogs and cats, by the way. Ha, ha, hah!—and then have her tell me he's very nice and interesting too. Did I?'

'There's nothing wrong with painting dogs and cats,' Kate said defensively. 'I only meant . . . How was I to know what he does for a living? Anyway, he paints proper pictures as well. Doesn't he?' she added, looking to Jenny for support.

Jenny smiled, nodded and sat back and kept quiet. She was enjoying this.

'You could tell just by looking at him what he does,' Lucy said confidently. 'Anyone with an ounce of . . . At least, I could.'

'Oh, you could! Of course you could. But a normal person is bound to have difficulty.'

'Well, he's not weird-looking, is he?' Lucy persisted. 'So he's not an experimental artist, like at Tate Modern, or somewhere. And he's not dressed in rags, and corduroy and things. So he's not penniless either. He paints, but he makes a living out of it. So he must paint what people want to buy. Right?'

'Portraits of dogs and cats?' Kate asked.

'Exactly!'

'Listen to Madame Maigret!' Kate invited, with a despairing look at Jenny.

'Oh, I am,' Jenny assured her. 'And it's absolutely fascinating.'

'I'm wasted on you two,' Lucy said unabashed. But she wasn't finished yet. 'Will is obviously slightly prosperous,' she continued. 'That means he paints things that sell in his own lifetime. That's always a plus. At least, I think so. Hence family portraits,

97

and the like.' She paused and looked round expectantly, as if waiting for the applause.

'Bravo!' Kate admitted.

'Actually,' Jenny added, 'I think he's fairly prosperous, even without selling his paintings. He lives in an absolutely enormous house that was built by his grandfather.'

'Lives alone?' Lucy demanded.

Jenny nodded.

'I knew it! I just knew it. He's been waiting all his life, Jen, for someone like you—someone exactly like you—to come along. You have been out with him, obviously?'

'A few times. We've had a meal together. That sort of thing. I've been to his house. He comes here.'

'Wonderful!' Lucy breathed. 'You've got him interested, Jen. Strike while the iron is hot, girl. That's my advice. What do you say, Kate?'

'Oh, yes! Yes, indeed. He'd make a wonderful catch.'

It was all too much. Jenny turned away, embarrassed now. 'I'm not sure how interested I am in him, though,' she said with a sigh. 'Not in the way you two mean, that is.'

'Well, you should be,' Lucy said severely. 'You're not getting any younger. None of us is. That old biological clock is ticking ever faster, you know. You want a family, don't you?'

'Who would like another coffee?' Jenny asked, desperate to change the subject. 'Or a glass of sherry, or white wine?'

'Another thing,' Lucy added, casting the last vestige of caution aside, 'if you marry Will, you won't have to bother with the shop. You won't need to.'

'That's enough!' Jenny said sharply. 'For your information, I have no marriage thoughts or plans at all. Not in relation to Will or anyone else. And, Lucy, I love my shop. I wouldn't give it up for anything. It's something I've wanted to do for a long time and now I can.'

After a moment's hesitation, the irrepressible Lucy said, 'But you don't know if you want Will?'

'No, I don't.'

'That's a pity.' Lucy glanced at the other two and added, 'There goes my chance of getting a free portrait of my cat. The kids, as well, sadly.'

Jenny stared at her, scandalised. Then Kate winked. Lucy fluttered her eyelids with mock innocence. And Jenny began to laugh.

The laughter became hysterical. Lucy threw a cushion at Kate, who responded in kind. Like old times, Jenny realised. Absolute pandemonium had broken out.

'You two!' Jenny gasped.

Then she, too, grabbed a cushion to wield.

'I know Lucy can be terrible,' Kate said later, 'but sometimes her instincts are right, you know. I've often found that. Maybe you should think seriously about Will. He obviously likes you a lot.'

'It's far too soon, Kate,' Jenny protested. 'He's a lovely man, I agree, but I hardly know him. Besides, I'm not sure he's interested in me anyway.'

'Oh, he is! Lucy and I are both sure of it. And you like him. So work at it. Reciprocate. Let him see the interest is mutual—or that it might be, in time. That's all we're saying. If you are interested, that is?'

'It's a long time since you and Pete split up. You should try again.'

Ah, yes! Pete. Jenny had almost forgotten about Pete and their engagement. It was another lifetime ago. Even before Mum had become so ill. Kate was so wrong if she thought that her broken relationship with Pete still bothered her.

On the other hand, she really didn't know about Will. Not in that sense, she didn't. She just thought of him as a friend. That's all he was so far. And it seemed enough.

'I don't wish to be rude, Kate, but . .'

'I know you want us to shut up! You didn't invite us here to be marriage guidance counsellors.'

'Well, I don't think I'd go so far as to tell you to shut up . . .'

'It's just that we want you to be settled, and to have a full and happy life. That's all.'

Jenny tried to relax and be philosophical

about it.

'I know you mean well, Kate. Of course I do. But I already have a full and happy life. At least, I think I do—in my view of what that means. I've got a home and the shop. I'm doing what I want to do, and I'm happy about it.

'Just because you and Lucy have husbands and, in her case, children, it doesn't mean everyone has to. Besides, there's plenty of time for me to think about marriage and children.'

'Of course there is!'

After a moment, Kate added, 'You're not forty yet, are you? And even then . . .'

'I'm thirty-three, for goodness' sake! Now drop the subject, please!'

'I will, I will!'

'Thank you. Anyway, you don't have children either.'

'But we are trying,' Kate said in a forlorn tone. 'We've been trying for ages.'

Jenny knew she wasn't the only one whose life might be considered incomplete by some and she gave Kate a hug. Then they both got on with washing and drying the pots, while Lucy went off to have a leisurely bath.

*　　*　　*

Despite what she'd said to her friends, Jenny was troubled. She felt that behind their

101

unwelcome opinions and advice there was something in what they'd been saying to her that struck a chord deep within her.

She did, eventually, want a family of her own. She always had done. Husband, children, and so on. The works. She wanted all that, just as Kate and Lucy and her own mother had wanted it. The difference was that they had been lucky enough to find someone to share their lives with. She had not. Rather, she had thought for a time she had, but in the end she hadn't. Not really. Pete and she had been wise to call it all off before the wedding day had arrived.

But just because she hadn't found the right person yet, that didn't mean she never would. Did it?

As for Will Renfrew, she hadn't really considered him in a romantic light. Or in any other light, for that matter. She had been far too busy settling into Cragley, sorting out the house and the shop, getting to know people and getting to know how to live in this new place. Enjoying it, too.

But now that she did stop to think about Will, she knew Kate and Lucy might well be right about some things. He did seem interested in her. She liked him, too. Maybe she should let him know his attentions were not unwelcome?

Except . . . Except . . . What? Well, to be honest, she didn't experience any great thrill when she was with him. She didn't long for him to hold her either. And she couldn't recall ever reaching out spontaneously to touch his arm or hug him, as she did sometimes with Tom, say. She just enjoyed being with Will and listening to him talk. Especially about his work. She enjoyed his company.

Maybe that was enough for grown-up people? Maybe that was all there was, or could be between mature people after the first flush of romance had faded?

She shook her head. She didn't know. Lucy would of course. And possibly even Kate would. But she wasn't going to ask them. There were limits to friendship.

An Invitation

After Kate and Lucy left, the house felt empty. And the next morning it was so quiet! It was unbelievable how full and noisy her two friends had made the place feel.

Jenny smiled to herself as she prepared her solitary breakfast.

It had been so good to see them both again, and they had packed so much into the few days they had spent together.

She hadn't wanted to close the shop, and Kate and Lucy had understood that, but even so, with Hannah's help, they had managed to

103

do and see plenty. And Lucy had quite fancied herself as a shopkeeper!

For a moment Jenny thought back to Dartford and to her old home. She'd experienced both good times and bad back there, and Kate and Lucy had always supported her no matter what.

But there was no going back, even if she wanted to, which she didn't. It had never been the same once Mum had gone.

And even if she could sell this place, she would never be able to afford a house back there now.

She wandered out into the garden where she was surprised to find Hannah hard at work.

'Hannah! Who gave you permission to pick my weeds?' she demanded. 'I wanted all those dandelions and thistles, and whatever else you've got in that plastic bag.'

Hannah grinned. 'We need to get the garden ready for spring.'

'Oh? We do, do we?'

'Definitely.' Hannah nodded and got back to work.

It seemed a strange time of year to be weeding, but the sun was shining, it was a warm day, and the garden needed it.

A tractor and plough might have made things easier, though. It was a long time since anyone had done any sort of real work in this garden.

Jenny smiled. 'It's going to take a lot of effort,' she observed, surveying the dense patches of nettles and thistles.

'Hard work never killed anyone,' Hannah pointed out sternly. 'Except our James, of course. It would do for him if he ever tried it.'

'Don't be so hard on him. He's only a man, and men don't know as much as women about hard work. So my mum used to say anyway.'

Jenny grabbed a clump of chickweed and worked side-by-side with Hannah for a few minutes until her back began to ache dangerously.

'That will have to do for now,' she puffed. 'I'm not used to hard work myself. Besides, I'll have to open the shop soon.'

They sat on a couple of old garden chairs for a moment.

'I didn't expect to see you here this morning, Hannah. It was a nice surprise.'

'I thought you might be feeling lonely.'

Jenny looked at her with surprise, touched by her concern. 'Now your friends have gone,' Hannah added.

'What a kind thought! Thank you. Actually, I was feeling a bit down in the dumps. The house has been so full of life the last few days, and we had such fun together.'

'Talking about old times, I expect,' Hannah said.

'Oh, yes! Quite a bit of that. It was good to see them both again.'

'I liked them both, especially Lucy. I wish I had friends like that.'

'You will. Of course you will! You probably have them already.'

'No.' Hannah shook her head. 'Mum was my best friend.'

Jenny winced. No-one spoke of it usually, but Annie's death had obviously left all her family terribly bereft. It was hard to imagine quite what an impact it must have had on poor Hannah.

'I miss my mum, too,' Jenny said quietly. 'She died not long ago.'

She looked up into Hannah's stricken face. Tears were threatening for both of them. She reached out to hold her.

'We'll just have to get used to it,' she said gently. 'They would want us to have happy lives, wouldn't they? Not to forget them, but to be happy even if they can't be with us. I think so, anyway.'

She felt Hannah nod agreement. She gently stroked the girl's hair until a kind of peace came over them both.

'Did you want to go back to Kent with Kate and Lucy?' Hannah asked.

'Not really.' Jenny had no hesitation. 'Not at all, actually. I'm here now.'

'Good.'

They sat together then until the sun moved behind the tree tops along the riverside. How good it is here, Jenny thought. How happy I

106

am to be here.

*　　*　　*

Later, Will dropped by. Jenny was pleased to see him. 'Have they gone?' he asked.
'I'm afraid so.'
'What a whirlwind!'
She laughed. 'That's exactly what they're like, aren't they? But it was lovely to see them both again and to have them here. I think they enjoyed themselves, too.'
'I'm sure they did.'
She regarded him fondly. 'And thank you, Will, for helping make it such a memorable visit. They enjoyed your company.'
'I liked them, too. They were good fun.' He stopped and looked around the shop. 'Much happening?'
'It's been not bad at all. I've had a few customers. Looking for Christmas presents mostly.'
He nodded. 'Trade picks up for most people, I think, in the run-up to Christmas. Not far away now, is it?'
It was true. A couple of weeks only. She couldn't believe she'd been in Cragley getting on for half a year already.
'What are you doing at Christmas, by the way?' Will asked. 'Anything special?'
'Me? Oh, I don't think so. I need to keep the shop open and busy. So I'll probably just

107

close for the two days. How about you?'

He shrugged. 'My married sister and her family want me to go to them in Manchester, or perhaps for them to come here. As usual,' he added.

'You're not keen to go to Manchester?'

'Not really.' He looked at her and added, 'How would you like to spend Christmas Day with me and my family at my place? Turkey, pudding, tree—the whole thing!'

'That's a nice idea, Will. Thank you.' She hesitated. 'Can I think about it and let you know? I've got so much going around in my head at the moment, I can't think straight.'

He approached her and took her hand. 'If you say yes,' he promised, 'we'll make it the most wonderful Christmas ever.' She smiled, and accepted the kiss he planted on her cheek.

Christmas Day

Late afternoon on Christmas Eve, just as Jenny was closing the shop, Hannah called round. 'Sorry I couldn't be here earlier. I had to help my dad.'

'No need to apologise, Hannah. You do more than enough around here.'

'Were you busy?'

'I was until lunch time but then it went quiet in the afternoon. I suppose I could have

108

closed then, but I stayed open just in case somebody was still searching for a last-minute present.'

'You didn't see James, then?'

'I didn't. Is that what he's doing? Shopping for last minute presents?'

Hannah nodded. 'He's the same every year. He doesn't get organised in time.'

Jenny hid a smile. Hannah's menfolk were always letting her down, one way or another. She was a hard taskmaster.

'It's a pity you can't come to our house on Christmas Day,' Hannah said ruefully.

Jenny wasn't sure. She knew Hannah could have liked her to be present, but she wasn't sure about the rest of the Laidler family. Besides, she was already committed.

'I'm sorry, Hannah. I accepted Mr Renfrew's invitation a week or two ago. I can't let him down, can I?'

Hannah shook her head. 'It's still a pity, though.'

'Well, maybe you could all come here on Boxing Day?'

'Can't. We have to go to Aunt Thelma's. We go there every year.'

'Well, some other time, then?'

Hannah hesitated and then said, 'Me and Dad are going to Midnight Mass tonight. Do you want to come with us?'

'Oh!' Jenny hadn't considered that possibility. She'd been too busy. But it suddenly seemed a nice idea. 'Where? The parish church?'

'St. Aidan's, yes. About eleven-fifteen we'll be going.'

'That would be lovely, Hannah. Are you sure your dad won't mind?'

'Oh, no. He told me to ask you'

'Well, thank you again.'

* * *

They came for her just after eleven. It was a frosty night and Hannah was well wrapped up against the cold. Tom wore a suit, which was a surprise. And no coat over it, which seemed rather bold.

'Goodness, Tom!' Jenny said. 'You look very smart, but won't you freeze?'

He just smiled. 'I'll be fine.'

'Dad doesn't feel the cold,' Hannah said. 'Not like me!'

'Well, you should be all right,' Jenny said to her. 'That looks a lovely warm coat.'

'It was my mum's.'

Jenny glanced at Tom.

'Annie would have wanted her to get some use out of it,' Tom said.

Jenny shut the door and they set off on the short walk across the green to the parish church.

It felt good to be in such company. She linked arms with Hannah and smiled happily

110

at Tom, who smiled back and took her other arm.

At the far side of the green, Jenny slipped slightly on the icy pavement. Tom's arm went round her and saved a fall. 'These shoes!' she muttered, smiling her thanks.

'You need to take care,' Tom said solemnly.

'You, too, Hannah.'

Not a thought for himself, mused Jenny, as he steered them both across the road and into the church.

* * *

It was a while since Jenny had last been in a church, but that night St. Aidan's seemed the right place to be. The perfect place to be.

She felt the majesty of the atmosphere as soon as they walked through the door.

There was a big attendance that night and she was thrilled to be amongst so many people she recognised from around the village. The organ sounded splendid and the choir was in good voice.

So, too, was the congregation and she soon found herself singing merrily alongside Hannah.

It felt good, she decided. It was good. She was sorry when the service ended and it was time to leave.

'Thank you so much for inviting me along,' she said to Tom and Hannah as they were about to part.

'Thank you for coming,' Tom said with great seriousness. Then he did a most unexpected, most unlike him sort of thing. He leaned forward and kissed her cheek. 'Happy Christmas!' he said softly.

'Happy Christmas!' she responded, in a daze.

*   *   *

Christmas Day was nice, too. Jenny was up early. She sorted out the presents she was leaving next door and the one she'd bought for Will. Then she listened to carols on the radio. Finally, it was time. She could get ready to go and join Will and his sister and her family for Christmas dinner.

Everything was beautiful. Will had excelled himself. He had thought of everything. Or, if he hadn't, his sister, Penny, had.

'I'm so glad to meet you at last,' Penny said, a bright smile lighting up her face. 'Will has told me everything about you. I feel I know you already, even though we haven't met.'

'I hope he's told you the truth!' Jenny said with an embarrassed laugh. 'That would be better than telling you everything.'

'Oh, yes,' Penny insisted. 'He's told me about your shop, and all the hard work you've put into it. How is it going, by the way?'

'Probably as well as could be expected. I

think that's the appropriate phrase.'

'Good! I'm so pleased. Now come and meet my family. Then I must join Will in the kitchen.'

Penny had a husband, a daughter and a son. Jenny liked them all. They were a nice family. And Will was a good host, as well as an excellent cook. So it turned out to be a lovely meal and an enjoyable day. Jenny was grateful she had been invited. Christmas Day was the one day in the year she wouldn't have wanted to be alone.

Yet . . . And yet she kept wondering as the afternoon wore on how the Laidlers were enjoying the day. She wondered what they were doing. She wondered if they liked the gifts she'd left for them. Somehow it felt wrong that she was here amongst strangers, apart from Will, rather than with the people she had become so used to seeing every day. Perhaps, she thought, she might see them briefly before the day was over.

*　　*　　*

Will walked her home that evening. He took her hand and gave it a squeeze. She smiled and thanked him again.

Outside her house, she said, 'I won't ask you in, Will. I'm so tired I'm going to fall asleep at any moment.'

'That's all right. I understand.'

He leaned forward to kiss her. She turned her head slightly so that his lips met her cheek. Then she gave his hand a final squeeze and turned towards her front door, relieved it had been so easy to avoid his advances, yet troubled that she had so instinctively done so.

Settling Down

After Christmas, as December turned into January, life settled down into a new pattern. Jenny welcomed it, and soon grew accustomed to the new routine. The stability suited her. She enjoyed it, especially everything to do with the shop.

Being her own boss and in charge of something she had created was becoming a satisfying experience.

She also enjoyed the contacts she was making amongst the local craftspeople.

And what a lot of local produce there was! More than she had ever suspected. At times the countryside seemed to be teeming with people making, crafting and collecting things. All sorts of interesting people were doing it, and her shop was fast becoming a meeting place for many of them.

It was a very different world to the one she had known for so long, but Jenny felt she was fitting into it nicely. She had never had such a wide circle of friends and acquaintances, even if fewer of them were customers than she would have liked.

'It's the coffee that does it,' Will told her, joking. 'That's what brings them in. The free coffee. People will travel miles for that and a gossip. Can I ask you to display my own business card, by the way?'

'Of course you can. I have a special panel that I use to display business cards.'

'So I noticed. Not a window?'

'No. I want to keep the windows clear. I don't want the place to look cluttered, like a junk shop.'

'A classy joint, eh? Well, it makes sense. Maybe you'll attract a more discerning customer.'

'More of any kind of customer would be very welcome at the moment'

Will smiled sympathetically. Then he stretched out in the wooden rocking chair strategically placed near the fireplace, where logs were quietly glowing.

'I have to go into Berwick this afternoon,' he said. 'Care to join me?'

'I'd love to, Will, but I can't. I can't close the shop.'

'Hannah?'

'Is at school,' said Jenny firmly, 'which is where she needs to be.'

Will nodded. 'This evening, then? Come up to the house. I'll make you a wonderful spaghetti bolognese.'

'That sounds nice, but isn't it your turn to come here for supper?'

'I don't know. Can't remember. And it doesn't matter anyway. You're busier than I am at the moment.'

'No new commissions?'

'Nothing much. I'm between things right now.'

She smiled. 'Then I'd love to come up tonight. Thank you.'

*   *   *

But after Will had gone she wondered if she'd been wise to accept his invitation. She had so much to do. She couldn't afford the time to be out as much in the evenings as Will seemed to like. Besides, she had seen rather a lot of him lately, and she wasn't sure that was such a good thing.

Also, she needed to see Hannah after supper. And Tom.

Rather, she *wanted* to see them, especially Tom. She'd seen so little of him since Christmas Eve. And she missed him.

Her thoughts returned to Will. She enjoyed his company. She liked listening to him. He could be so amusing. He was such a repository of local information, as well. He knew everything and everyone in and around the district. He was such a good friend.

And he liked her. She knew that. She wasn't totally insensitive, whatever Kate thought. Maybe Kate and Lucy were right, though. Maybe she should respond more eagerly to his approaches. She could do a lot worse than throw in her lot with Will.

She sighed and poked the fire, causing a shower of sparks to leap from the logs and fly up the chimney like demented spirits. She just wasn't sure how she felt about Will. Somehow she just wasn't. Even now.

Natural caution, she supposed. And surely caution wasn't such a bad thing, was it? She'd been single so long. She didn't need to rush into things now. In time, perhaps, she would feel ready to contemplate a future with Will. And then she would let him know. Quite clearly. Just as Kate and Lucy had advised. Not now, though. Not yet. The shop needed all her attention until it was fully off the ground.

*   *   *

She called next door to see Hannah before she visited Will. Tom led the way into the kitchen. 'Come in, Jenny. I'll just give her a shout. She's washing her hair or something.'

'Oh, don't bother her, Tom. I'll catch her another time.'

'Sure?'

She nodded. 'I'm in a rush. I'm going to

117

Will's for supper.'

Tom nodded but didn't comment. 'No time for a coffee?'

She hesitated, but not for long. 'A quick one, perhaps.'

He picked up the kettle. He was looking so well, she thought. Happy, even. Things must be going so much better for him.

'I'm glad to see you've set up your workshop in the shed,' she told him.

'Oh, yes. I'm starting to get quite a lot of work coming in now. I can't thank you enough for letting me have the shed.'

She shrugged. 'I don't need it. Not much of it, anyway.'

He made the coffee and sat down across the table from her.

He gazed at her and smiled.

'What?' she said. 'What have I done now?'

'Nothing,' he said, shaking his head and laughing. 'Not a thing'

She grinned. She couldn't help it. 'You hadn't used to laugh,' she pointed out. 'Not while I was around anyway.'

'Maybe I didn't have much to laugh about.'

'And you do now?'

He stopped laughing and nodded. 'Now I do,' he said.

He touched the back of her hand briefly with his fingertips. She shivered and looked down.

She wondered all that night if she was right

118

about what she had seen in his eyes and heard in his voice.

Hard Times

Happy as Jenny had been with the way things were going in the shop, January turned out not to be so good for business. The weather became cold and grey, and so did Jenny's spirits. Customers were few. Sales even fewer. But the bills kept on coming in.

Will tried to cheer her up, but with little success. As the money—her precious money! kept on pouring away, she had little appetite for Will's tales of the heroic struggle artists such as himself had to endure.

'I've a family portrait to do just now. And the children won't sit still,' he complained. 'Not for a moment. Their mother threatens them, cajoles them, punishes them, but all to no avail. With Christmas and presents behind them, nothing in the world will make them sit still to have their portrait painted.'

'You can hardly blame them,' Jenny pointed out. 'Even the Queen must find it an unbearable ordeal at times.'

'Perhaps so. But the cats and dogs are no better.'

'Will!' Jenny cried with exasperation. 'Dogs and cats can't be expected to sit still for you.'

'Perhaps not.'

He looked unpersuaded.

'Anyway,' she added in an emollient tone, 'who are all these people with money to spend on portraits. Minor aristocrats?'

'You'd be surprised. Farming families keeping up a tradition. Newly successful business people, especially older gentlemen with young, second wives.'

Jenny laughed and shook her head, wondering how she was ever going to get him out of the house.

'I even suspect I'm laundering the money of the occasional crime boss,' he added darkly. 'Not all my clients seem to be discerning patrons of the arts. What?' he added.

'Oh, I'm sorry, Will!' Jenny stifled a yawn.

'Tired, or just bored?'

She gave a rueful smile. 'Exhausted, I'm afraid. I think I'm going to have to ask you to leave. I have such a lot to do, and I really am very tired. Do you mind?'

'Of course not.' He got up out of the chair. 'You're a very busy lady. I know that. And some things won't wait.'

She nodded, relieved to have got him moving.

'How about Thursday evening? Fancy a trip to the theatre in Berwick? Think you can make it?'

'The Maltings?'

He nodded.

'What's on?'

'A film—a French film about the life of Edith Piaf.'

'Oh, yes. I read about that. Yes, I'd love to go.'

'Good. There's something I'd like to talk to you about as well. Ask you about, rather. About us. The future and so on.' He stopped and looked slightly embarrassed. 'When you're in the mood, that is. Not . . . not when you're too tired.'

She nodded. She could guess what he wanted to say to her and she was thankful he was postponing the conversation. He was right. She wasn't in the mood. Not at all. Not now. She was grateful he'd realised that. She was grateful she didn't have to say anything more.

But she knew the conversation was merely being postponed, and she also knew it was one she didn't really want to have. Not yet, at least. If ever, she thought despondently. Why, oh why couldn't he just leave it? Why couldn't they just continue to be friends?

*   *   *

Will went on his way, and she was alone again. Alone with her account books and her worries about the shop. Yet even that was better than enduring Will's amusing stories that for some time now had ceased to enthral her.

Oh, what was wrong with her? How could she think like that? How could she be so glad to see the back of him?

Well, perhaps it wasn't so much of a mystery. It was because of the shop, she decided. Until, and unless, things improved, she wasn't going to be very interested in seeing anyone who wasn't a genuine customer. She couldn't afford to be.

She regretted now that she'd accepted Will's theatre invitation. She'd only done so to get him out of the house. Maybe she could conjure up an excuse and change her mind?

But . . . Dear Will! She was so lucky to have such a good friend. He was such a lovely man. And she knew it. She did. It was just that she was so tired these days. And so worried.

The door bell dragged her away from her miserable thoughts.

She glanced at the clock. Eight-thirty. Who could it be at this time of night?

*   *   *

'Hello, Tom! I didn't expect to see you.'

'Hannah said you weren't feeling so good. I just wondered if there was anything I could do?'

He looked concerned. She gave a wan smile. 'Come in, Tom!' He followed her inside and shut the door. She led the way into the kitchen. 'Coffee?'

122

'I'll not stay, Jenny. Not if you're not well. Is there anything I can help you with?'

'I'm just tired, Tom. That's all.' She switched the kettle on. 'Worn out, more like it. Too many worries. But it's good to see you,' she added with a smile.

'Worries? The shop, you mean?'

She nodded. 'There haven't been many customers since Christmas. But the bills keep on coming.'

'Things will pick up in the spring,' he said. 'Don't worry.'

She smiled. 'I hope so.'

'I could find you some customers,' he suggested. 'Bang a few heads together, drag them in. Make them buy a few things. How would that be?'

It was absurd but she began to laugh. 'Oh, Tom!' she said, 'I feel better already.'

Trouble For James

A few days later, Jenny turned in alarm as Hannah burst into the shop and flopped on to a chair. The poor girl looked very upset.

'What's wrong, Hannah? Hannah!'

'Nothing. Nothing's wrong.'

Jenny didn't pursue it. She studied her visitor for a moment. Then she quietly turned her back and continued checking through the

123

invoices she had been looking at.

The big clock on the wall ticked and tocked. Outside, the wind tugged at the edges of the window. A timber lorry passed by, and the whole building trembled. Hannah sniffled. Jenny stood up and quietly went over to her. She knelt down and gave her a hug, and gently smoothed the hair away from the girl's eyes, eyes that were brimming with tears.

'It's that woman!' Hannah blurted out. 'She's here again.'

Jenny was puzzled. 'What woman? I don't understand.'

'Her from the council!'

Ah! Jenny was less puzzled now. The Education Welfare Officer, or whatever her correct title was, must have come to see Tom again about Hannah's truancy. She'd heard about her before.

'But you've been attending school regularly lately, haven't you? What's the problem?'

'It's not me. It's James. He's the problem. I told him off about it! Dad told him as well.'

'So what's happened now?'

'She wants James to sign something. She says he'll be up in court next time if he doesn't. Then it'll be . . . custody? Is that the right word?'

Jenny nodded. 'It could be.'

This sounded a worrying development. The authorities must have tired of speaking and writing to James, and to Tom. It was hard to

124

blame them.

'That woman's really mean,' Hannah insisted. 'She says James does nothing, causes trouble all the time, and . . .'

'Is she at your house now?'

Hannah nodded.

Jenny guessed Tom would be out of his depth faced with officialdom backed up by legal powers especially if it was a woman! He would be too polite. He wouldn't feel he could argue with her.

'Can you look after the shop for a few minutes, Hannah?'

'Yes. But why? What are you going to do?'

'I'm not sure,' Jenny confessed. 'But I'm going to do something. I'm going to see if I can help. There must be something I can do.'

*　　*　　*

She didn't bother knocking or ringing the door bell. She walked straight in and made her way to the kitchen, the family's usual gathering place.

They were there, the three of them, gathered round the big farmhouse table. Tom himself, looking worried and dispirited, James, in his most sullen and unco-operative mood, and a smartly dressed woman, mid-thirties, in a black suit and white blouse, her blonde hair cut severely short.

'Hello, everyone!' Jenny said brightly.

125

'Sorry to interrupt.' They all looked at her, puzzled.

'Jenny!' Tom said, getting to his feet, trying hard to smile a welcome.

'Hello, Tom. Hello, James. Oh, I'm sorry! I didn't realise you had a visitor?'

She gazed at the woman and waited expectantly.

'This is Miss Gregg from the County Council,' said Tom.

'The Education Welfare Service,' Miss Gregg corrected him. 'And you are . . .?'

'Oh, I'm Jenny Morrison from the shop next door.'

'Actually, Miss Morrison, we're having an important meeting. I wonder if you would mind coming back later?' said Miss Gregg, rather rudely since she was in someone else's house, Jenny thought.

'Miss Gregg's come about James,' Tom said quickly.

'Oh, I won't hold you up!' Jenny fixed a bright smile firmly in place. 'I just wanted a quick word with James. Then I'll be on my way.'

'Perhaps you can . . .' Miss Gregg began.

Jenny ignored her and turned to James. 'The computer's down again, James. I'm hoping you'll be able to come and sort it out for me, like you did last time. Are you terribly, terribly busy? Oh, and yes, I did remember to plug it in and switch it on! So that's not the

126

problem this time.'

James stared at her. Bewilderment turned quickly to amusement.

'I expect it's the anti-virus software,' he said. 'It'll be interfering with the start-up programme. What you need is . . .'

He launched into a technical explanation that she didn't even begin to understand but she continued smiling and hoped Miss Gregg was impressed. She certainly was herself.

'I know you've got a lot on at the moment what with helping your Dad with his work and so on,' Jenny said eventually. 'Hannah told me. But when do you think you might be able to take a look?'

'Maybe later on tonight?' he said. 'I could have a quick look? See if we need to order new software. Or spare parts for the machine. You might need some more memory capacity. If it's going to be a big job I'll not be able to get it sorted straight away, but with a bit of luck it won't be.'

Jenny closed her eyes for a moment on Miss Gregg's blind side. Perfect! James was playing his part beautifully.

'The computer's so important to me,' she said, turning to address the visitor. 'My business is totally dependent on it. I don't know what I'd do without this young man to help me out!'

Miss Gregg gave Jenny a cool look. Then she glanced at James. 'You didn't mention any

127

of this,' she said severely. 'I wasn't aware you had this . . . interest. Or that you'd been helping your father.'

James shrugged. 'You never asked.'

Jenny smiled to herself and turned away. 'Thank you!' she called, heading for the door. 'Sorry to interrupt.'

Fingers crossed, she thought to herself as she left the house. Fingers crossed and chin up!

A Quiet Word

The bell rang as someone entered the shop. Jenny straightened up from the box she was unpacking and turned to see who it was.

'Hello!' called Miss Gregg.

'Oh, hello. Can I help you?'

Miss Gregg didn't look quite so severe now. She was smiling, in fact. 'That was very nicely done,' she said.

'I beg your pardon?'

'Your intervention on behalf of James Laidler. You carried it off well.'

She seemed friendly, rather than sarcastic, and Jenny began to relax. 'I'm pleased you think so,' she said.

'Oh, I do! It may well have the effect I believe you intended.'

Jenny nodded and smiled. 'That would be

128

excellent. Can I offer you coffee, or tea?'

'Coffee would be very welcome. It smells lovely. Thank you.'

'Have a seat. Please.'

Miss Gregg sat down and yawned. 'I'm so tired all the time,' she complained. 'I don't know what's wrong with me these days.'

'Stress, probably,' Jenny suggested, 'if you have many youngsters like James to deal with.'

'Oh, there are a lot worse than him, believe me!'

'I'm glad you see it that way.'

Miss Gregg took the mug Jenny held out to her. Her fingers traced the twisting vine curling away from the handle. 'This is pretty.'

'Locally made,' Jenny said. 'Like all my stuff.'

'And such lovely flowers! They won't be local, though, not at this time of year.'

'From Jersey, I think,' Jenny said, glancing at the latest bouquet, which had arrived that morning.

Miss Gregg nodded and then sighed deeply: 'All the times I've visited James and his father, I never knew about the boy's interest in computers. It's not surprising, of course, in a lad his age, but neither of them ever saw fit to mention it.'

'He's good,' Jenny said. 'Genuinely interested, too.'

'So I gather, thanks to you.'

Jenny smiled and shrugged the compliment

aside, feeling a little embarrassed. 'Will it help, knowing that?'

'Oh, yes. I really do think so. It could save his bacon.'

Miss Gregg shook her head and chuckled. 'But why didn't he say something? He just sits and sulks usually! I can't get anything out of him.'

'Is that so unusual, with teenage boys in trouble?'

Miss Gregg laughed. 'Point taken. I suppose not, no.' They smiled at one another.

Jenny poured more coffee. As she did so, she gathered her thoughts and tried to put them into words.

'I think I know James and his sister have had a difficult time since their mother died. Tom, too. He's done his best for the kids, bless him, but you can't be both mother and father, however hard you try. It's impossible.'

'You're right. Absolutely.' Miss Gregg took a sip of coffee. 'Anyway, I'm going to arrange for James to do some IT courses. He seems pleased at the prospect. I'm daring to hope this will make him turn the corner. Maybe even get him back to school.'

'Wonderful!' Jenny smiled with delight. 'And the trouble he's in?'

'Oh, it's nothing much. He's just been a bit lippy to one or two people. I'm going to draw up a contract with him, to make sure of his commitment. If he fulfils his side of the bargain by attending the courses then his slate will be wiped clean.'

Jenny felt immensely satisfied. Her intervention really did seem to have helped.

'With so many youngsters like James,' Miss Gregg added, 'it's a struggle to do anything with them. They're not interested in anything, a lot of them. James is different it seems. I can see that now. And I'm glad.'

She put down her mug and glanced at the clock. 'Oh, dear! I must fly.'

'I'm so happy it's working out,' Jenny said shyly.

'You're a very kind and wise woman,' said Miss Gregg. 'Thank you so much for what you've done. And, between you and me, I'm not really such an ogre, you know. It's just a difficult job at times.'

Jenny nodded. 'I can see that.'

The welfare officer took a last glance around and added, 'I do hope your shop does well. You deserve it.'

Jenny smiled with pleasure. 'Thank you,' she said.

A Problem Shared

Kate was wonderful. So empathetic. No need to spell things out to her, she understood straight away.

131

'You're having second thoughts?' she suggested.

'Well . . .' Jenny hesitated. 'Not exactly. But . . .'

'Why don't you come and stay with us for a few days, Jen?' Suddenly it seemed a good idea.

'I could do with a break,' she admitted. 'Things have been getting on top of me a bit. But the shop . . .'

'Put a notice on the door,' Kate said firmly. 'CLOSED FOR ONE WEEK. That will do it.'

She supposed it would. The occasional customer, if serious, would come back. Besides, she had seen other businesses in the area doing the same thing. People had to have holidays. And this slack time of year was the sensible time to take them.

'Ted won't mind me coming to visit?'

'Ted? Of course not! Ted will adore having two women to entertain him.'

Jenny smiled. Kate was probably right.

'I'd certainly like to come, Kate, but I don't know when.'

'Next week,' Kate said firmly. 'Yes?'

'All right,' Jenny said reluctantly, laughing. 'I'll be there next week somehow!'

*   *   *

Kate and Ted lived on a smart new estate. They had only been there a year or two, but it

132

seemed to suit them fine.

'We'll not be here for ever, of course,' Kate said, as she pulled into the drive after picking Jenny up at the station, 'but it's convenient for now.'

'And ideally?' Jenny said. 'Eventually?'

'Oh, a cottage with roses round the door. And a three-car garage for the Bentley, the Maserati and the Range Rover.'

'So you'll be here for a little while longer?'

Kate grinned as she opened her door and Jenny followed, admiring the pocket-handkerchief sized lawn complete with thistles and dandelions.

'I must tell the gardener about that,' Kate said, noticing Jenny's interest. 'When I see him next. He doesn't like weeding.'

'That's Ted, is it?'

'It's certainly not me!'

They were busy people, Kate and Ted. Both worked somewhere in the city, though not in the kind of jobs that were ever likely to provide funds for a cottage with roses round the door, or the rest of it.

*   *   *

'Jenny!' Ted cried, as they entered the hall. 'You've returned to us.'

'Not for long, though,' Kate said firmly.

'Hello, Ted!' said Jenny with a smile. 'How are you?'

133

'The same as ever. Just the same. Come and tell me about the frozen North. Should we follow your example? Have you changed your mind? Or what?'

Laughing, Jenny allowed herself to settle into the warm and cosy atmosphere. They were good friends, Kate and Ted, and good hosts. It was lovely to see them again. Sadly, this was a week when Lucy and her family were away visiting relations. But there would be other times to see them. Meanwhile, here she was—relaxing with old chums!

* * *

That first evening Ted was eager to hear about *the business,* as he called it. Or *the shop,* as Jenny and Kate preferred. Jenny explained the situation, and her current problems.

'So basically,' Ted suggested, 'you've just started up at the wrong time of year? In a place like that—however lovely it is in the summer—you're not going to get many customers over the winter months, are you?'

'I suppose not,' Jenny agreed reluctantly. 'I had hoped to get *some,* though. And I did well in the period leading up to Christmas.'

'Of course you did! So did M&S and Tesco. But after Christmas, retailers do tend to suffer. Everyone's spent up by then.' Put like that it was so obviously true.

'You could close down for the winter

134

months?' Kate suggested. 'Do something else get a job even. Or go abroad.'

'Oh, I don't want to do that.'

'Or,' Ted said thoughtfully, 'you could stay right there, right where you are, and see if you can earn yourself some extra income doing something else.'

'Doing what, though?'

'I'll let you know!' Ted said, laughing.

'Coffee anyone?' Kate said. 'Then you can tell Ted all about Cragley, and me about that lovely man who's so devoted to you. Will, isn't it? Has he proposed yet?'

Jenny had been set to talk about Tom and the twins, and how they had all been helping each other. Instead, she told them about Will. That was what Kate wanted to hear, after all. In doing so, she managed not to say she had been fearing a proposal for some time—and didn't know what she would do about it, if and when it came.

＊　　＊　　＊

Kate returned to the subject after Ted had left them alone. 'I don't think you finished telling me about Will?'

Jenny laughed awkwardly. 'There's not much more to tell. You've met him. He hasn't changed.'

'Yes, but are you getting together with him? That's what I mean.'

'Oh, I know what you mean, Kate. The truth is . . . Well, no. Nothing's changed in that respect. We're good friends, and he's a nice bloke.'

'But?'

'Oh, Kate! It's too soon for anything else. We're not romantically involved or anything. At least, I'm not. But we might be, in time, I suppose. You know how these things work. You know better than me—all the experience you've had!'

'I have no idea what you mean,' Kate said, chuckling and fluttering her eyelashes. 'No idea at all.'

'No, of course you don't. Now can we please change the subject?'

'Certainly. It still seems a pity, though,' Kate added wistfully. 'I was looking forward to shopping for a new hat.'

On one level Jenny was irritated with her friend. She had no right to be poking around so persistently into such private matters. On the other hand . . . Well, what were friends for? What else could she have expected, especially of Kate?

'Let's go into town,' Kate suggested. 'Would you like to do that? Do some shopping?'

'Oh, yes please! I thought you'd never ask.'

Coming Home

She knew now what she must do. She had dillied and dallied for far too long. Lost her way and ...

She smiled ruefully. It had taken her short break away from Cragley for her to see where her future lay. They hadn't pressed. Not seriously. But somehow being with them, in her old haunts and out of Cragley, had allowed her to see things more clearly. She had needed the space and time.

Kate had been disappointed that she was leaving so soon. 'I must go, Kate. Really I must.'

Jenny and her friend were at the station, saying goodbye.

'Of course you must.' Kate sighed. 'And I must go back to work, I suppose. Back to the dreary round.'

'You don't mean that.'

'Don't I? Perhaps not. But sometimes I do. Then I remember I need to pay for all the retail therapy I undertake.'

Jenny smiled. 'Come and visit me again, Kate. Both of you, you and Ted. Or come again with Luce. I'd love to see you all again'

'I'd like to.'

'Anytime. In the spring, maybe?'

'Will there be lambs and daffodils and

things?' Kate asked wistfully.

'Lots of them, probably. There's bound to be.'

'I'm on my way!'

They hugged one another on the platform. Then Kate was gone. She couldn't abide farewells, she said, or King's Cross either. Jenny smiled after her until she had disappeared into the crowd. Then she got aboard the train.

*   *   *

And now, as the train sped northwards across the dreary flatlands of middle England, she felt both joy and apprehension. She was so glad to be going home—and it was home now. She was happy to be returning to Northumberland, to Cragley, to her home, to her shop. And to the people she knew there. They were her life now.

The shop remained a problem, of course. Or, rather, the poor trade at the moment did. But it would pick up as spring approached. Ted had said it would, and he knew about these things.

She knew it, too, of course. But it was good to have it confirmed.

In the meantime, until it did pick up, there were things she could do. Ted had given her some ideas about that, and she had had some of her own. There was plenty for her to consider, and to try.

It wasn't really the shop she was apprehensive about now, however. It was the other side of her life, the side that Kate was so interested in. The people side.

She was going to talk to Will. It was time. Past time, probably. She couldn't leave things up in the air any longer. It wasn't fair to him, apart from anything else. Anyway, her mind was made up now. Dear Will! She sighed and smiled, as she anticipated seeing him again.

She needed to talk to Tom, too, she thought reluctantly. And the twins. She hoped James had stuck to his new role and direction. She really did hope so. He was a far better boy than at first she had feared. A good boy, really, even if it had taken her a while to realise it.

And Hannah. She couldn't wait to see Hannah again and hear about what she had been doing.

Then she allowed herself to think of Tom. She was looking forward to seeing him again, too. Of course she was. She liked watching him making things in the workshop. In fact she just liked being near him. If only . . .

Forget it, my girl! She admonished herself sharply. Tom had his life and she had hers. Good lives, too. Both of them. Lives to be thankful for.

They had both known unhappiness and survived. Now it was up to each of them to

139

make the most of what they had, which was a lot. She knew that.

She could count her blessings as well as the next person. She wasn't a silly young girl any longer, if she ever had been. Mum would have been proud of her, and pleased for her. Dad, too, probably, though he had died so young she couldn't really remember him. Just his smile, and his voice. He would have been pleased for her, too. They both would. She knew that. Well, she hoped they would.

* * *

Will met her at the station in Berwick. He looked so distinguished, she thought fondly as she approached him. Such a lovely smile, too. He looked so pleased to see her.

'Will! It's lovely to see you. Thank you so much for remembering to come for me.'

He laughed and gave her a hug. She brushed his cheek with her lips.

'How are you?' he demanded, stepping away as if to see if she'd changed at all and gazing expectantly at her. 'You decided to come back?'

'Oh, Will! Of course I did. Cragley is home now, not Dartford.'

'I'm so glad. The village hasn't been the same without you.'

'Of course it has, silly! But thank you so much for coming to meet me.'

He grabbed her bag. She let him take it, and linked her arm in his.

'How was the journey?' he added, as they set off for the car.

'Wonderful! Do you know, it only took three hours. I can hardly believe it. The length of England in so little time.'

'So your friends are not really so far away, are they?'

'Not at all,' she said, wondering if he'd really been worried that she wouldn't return.

They reached the car. Will opened up, stored her bag and saw her inside.

'For you,' he said then, handing her a bouquet of flowers.

'Oh, Will! Thank you so much. They're lovely. But you shouldn't. You spend far too much on flowers for me.' He laughed and threw her a strange look.

She admired the bouquet and turned to lay it on the back seat. 'I've never thanked you for all the flowers,' she said, as he started the engine. 'It's very sweet of you.'

He chuckled. 'Well, if that's a hint . . .' He glanced at her and added, 'If I'd known they would make you so happy I'd have sent you more.'

It was her turn to laugh.

'Oh, I like them coming to the door so unexpectedly,' she said airily. 'It's always so deliciously mysterious.'

'I must remember that. Maybe I can do it

141

by internet. You can do so much that way these days.'
'I'm sure you can,' she said, giving him a puzzled glance.
'Next stop home!' he said.
'I can't wait.'

*   *   *

'I must leave you for now I'm afraid,' Will said, as he dropped her off. 'I've a client to see. A commission.'
'That's good.'
He grimaced. 'There are things I would rather be doing today.'
'Priorities, Will. Priorities!'
'I suppose so.' He shrugged. Then he looked at her and added, 'I don't suppose . . . ?'
'Not now, Will. Can we talk later? I'm so tired. And I want to get inside.'
'Sure.'
But he looked so disappointed that she paused. 'Will?'
He looked at her and said, 'Jenny, will you . . .'
'No, Will.' She couldn't help herself now. 'I'm ever so sorry, but it wouldn't work'
He nodded, cleared his throat and said, 'Sure?'
'I am, yes. It's not what I want, and I wouldn't be right for you, anyway.'
142

It took a moment. But eventually he smiled and said, 'You should let me be the judge of that.'

Then he turned and walked away.

She was sad for a few moments. But mostly she was relieved. Finally, she had been able to say what she had long dreaded saying, and she knew it was for the best for both of them.

An Accident

It was good to be home. The place still felt lived in, even though she'd been away for a week. Hannah had been putting the heating on each night to make sure the house didn't cool too much.

Jenny hoped she would see her before the day ended. She had a gift for her, as well as wanting to thank her.

But she didn't see anyone that first evening. She had thought Hannah or Tom might have popped round but concluded that they must be busy. She wasn't too disappointed, though. She really was tired. The travelling and the visiting had worn her out, in a pleasant way.

She made herself some scrambled eggs and a pot of tea, and afterwards she had a bath and went to bed. It wasn't long before sleep came.

The next morning she was up early, ready to make a determined start. Soon after eight she was in the shop, working.

She began by opening the mail that had accumulated. There was nothing terribly interesting, but she was pleased to see a letter of apology from a small company that had sent different vases to the ones she'd ordered. They were concerned. That was good. She would use them again.

Hannah put in a very brief appearance, en route to catch the school bus.

'Nothing happened while you were away,' she called from the doorway. 'Everything's all right. I just wanted to tell you.'

'Hannah! Come on in.' Jenny smiled and added, 'It's lovely to see you. How are you, dear?'

'All right.'

'And Dad and James?'

'They're all right too. I have to go now'

'Oh, yes. You don't want to be late. Will you come round when you get home?'

'I might.'

Hannah turned and stared at the bouquet of flowers that Will had given to Jenny the day before. 'Where did they come from?'

Jenny smiled. 'They're lovely, aren't they? More flowers from my admirer.'

Hannah stared at them. 'I don't think so,'

144

she said, shaking her head. 'He hasn't had time.'

'Who hasn't had time?'

'It doesn't matter,' Hannah said. 'Forget I said anything.'

'Will Renfrew gave them to me.'

'Mr Renfrew?'

'Yes. When he collected me from the station.'

Hannah studied them a moment longer, without further comment. Then she turned and left, leaving Jenny even more puzzled.

*   *   *

Shortly after eleven o'clock, an elderly lady from the village came in, looking for a birthday card for her grandson.

'I do have cards, Mrs Ord,' Jenny told her, 'but they're not proper birthday cards.'

'How do you mean?'

'Well, I don't have any with birthday messages on them, or the age of the person either.'

'What good are they, then?'

Jenny smiled. 'They're pretty, Mrs Ord! Isn't that enough?'

Without touching them, the old lady looked at the cards Jenny placed before her and said, 'Well, he can't read anyway. He's only two. He just likes pictures really.'

'What sort of pictures?'

145

'What have you got?'

Jenny smiled again. Easier to say what she hadn't got.

'Tell you what, Mrs Ord. Why don't you have a look for yourself? See if you can find anything suitable, while I finish putting the coffee on.'

She busied herself with the coffee maker. Mrs Ord started looking through the card collection. They were mostly postcards—arty cards.

Jenny wondered if she ought to think about stocking a range of birthday cards, and other celebration cards as well. She wouldn't sell a lot but there could be a steady trade.

'I'll have this one with the swans on,' Mrs Ord decided eventually, after considering one with cats, and another with cocker spaniels.

'Oh, yes. The swans on the river at Berwick.'

Mrs Ord nodded. 'He likes birds.'

'He should like that card, then. Everyone loves swans.'

Mrs Ord agreed. Then she added, 'You've been on holiday, have you? I noticed the shop was closed?'

'Yes. I went to visit friends in Kent.'

'Nice. You won't have heard the news, then?'

'What news, Mrs Ord?'

'About Tom Laidler?'

Jenny looked up. 'What do you mean?

146

What's happened?'

'The accident.'

'What accident? Mrs Ord?'

'He had an accident at work. Something fell on him, or he fell down or something. The paramedics had to take him to hospital.'

Jenny felt a tightness in her chest. She stood still, trying not to panic.

'He's not too bad, though. He's back home now, I believe.'

* * *

As soon as she could get rid of Mrs Ord, Jenny closed the shop and rushed next door. James answered her ring at the bell. 'Hi! How are you doing?'

'I've just heard about the accident, James.' Jenny said hurriedly. 'How's your dad?'

'Oh, he's all right. Are you coming in?'

'Is he in bed?'

'At this time of day?' James chuckled. 'He's in the kitchen.'

He would be in a wheelchair, probably, thought Jenny. Or one of those special beds. It would be easier to have it downstairs. More convenient. James and Hannah couldn't be rushing up and down the stairs all day.

Tom was actually sitting in an ordinary kitchen chair. 'Jenny! Hannah said you were back. How . . .'

'Never mind that, Tom. How are you? I just

147

found out about the accident. Mrs Ord . . .'

She stopped, breathless. realising Tom looked pretty normal. In one piece, at least.

'I thought it was funny no-one came round when I got home,' she continued slowly. 'Then Mrs Ord told me. How are you? What happened, actually?'

She stopped again.

He held up a hand. There was a thick bandage on his thumb. 'I had to have six stitches in it,' he said, eyes twinkling. Jenny stared, aghast. 'Is that all?' she demanded.

He nodded. 'How bad did you want me to be?'

Relief flooded through her. 'Oh, you fool!' she snapped, more to herself than to him.

'Steady on! I cut it. That's all. Had to go to hospital in Berwick.'

'But Mrs Ord said the ambulance . . .'

'I couldn't drive myself, could I?'

'Oh, Tom!'

She laughed and closed her eyes for a moment. 'I was so worried.'

'About what? Me?'

She laughed again and rushed to plant a kiss on his cheek. He hugged her. 'I'm all right,' he said. 'Don't worry about me. It's good to see you back,' he added.

'It's good to be back,' she murmured.

She closed her eyes and stayed where she was, glad to be so close to him, happy to have him hold her. He kept hold.

'How silly of me,' she said eventually. 'I thought . . . Oh, that Mrs Ord!'

'A right doom-monger, isn't she?'

Jenny nodded, but she was no longer upset or unduly bothered about Mrs Ord. Or the accident. Or Tom's health. Especially when he kissed her.

A Family Business

'So you've got a poorly finger?' He nodded and grinned at her. 'Anything else wrong with you?'

'Not a thing.'

'Sure?'

'Sure.'

'I'm so glad,' She laughed ruefully and shook her head. 'That Mrs Ord! What about Hannah? Is anything wrong with her?'

'Hannah? No. She's fine. Moody, but fine.'

'She seemed so . . . so distant this morning. I couldn't understand it.'

'Don't worry about it.'

'About what? Don't worry about what?'

Tom looked awkward for a moment.

'What is it, Tom? What are you not telling me?' She pulled away a little, so she could see his face more clearly. 'Is it James again?'

He shook his head. 'James is fine, too.'

'Tom!'

149

He gazed at her and shrugged apologetically. 'It's nothing.'

'Tom!'

He reached a decision. 'OK, then. You want to know the truth? Here it is. Hannah thinks you'll leave. She thinks you're going to go back to Kent.'

She stared at him.

'We all do,' he added with a shrug. 'We've been worried. Upset.'

'About me?' she said wonderingly. 'Tom! I had a week's break. I visited Kate and her husband. They're old friends.'

'I know, but ...'

'That's all, Tom.'

He shrugged again. 'She thought you wouldn't come back, and even if you did ...'

She was puzzled, as well as happy. She stared at him until what he was saying sank in.

'Poor girl. I must talk to her.'

'If you would.'

'You were all worried?' she said slowly.

He nodded.

'You, too, Tom?' she whispered, hardly daring to say it.

'Very much,' he said huskily, his face flushed.

'Why would you worry?'

'Why do you think?' He smiled and looked embarrassed. 'I'm very fond of you, Jenny. I'm not much good with words, but a man can have hope, can't he?'

'Hope, Tom? What do you mean?'
'Well, I know you're soft on Will Renfrew. Why wouldn't you be? He's a good-looking bloke with a lot to offer. Still . . . I hoped that if it didn't work out . . . One day, maybe.'
Her heart was pounding. She held her breath. 'Tom, I . . .'
'I know, I know! Silly, isn't it? But even if it is silly to think like that, I wouldn't want you leaving.'
Somehow, through all this, the answer to a little mystery revealed itself. She guessed now why Hannah had been so puzzled.
'Tom, have you been sending me flowers?'
He shrugged.
'Tom?'
'Once or twice, maybe,' he said diffidently.
She wrapped her arms round him and hugged him. 'You wonderful man!' she murmured. 'And all this time I thought you couldn't possibly be interested in me.'
He smiled and hugged her back. They kissed again, and she felt the thrill of being kissed by the man she wanted to do just that.
'I'm not soft on Will Renfrew, as you put it,' she said moments later. 'He's a friend, that's all.'
'I thought . . .'
'And I told him so yesterday, when he brought me home. You, and Hannah and James, are who I want to be with, Tom.'
He shook his head and hugged her with

delight. They gazed at each other with wonder.

'That's what I want, as well,' Tom said. 'You here with me. But I never thought it could possibly happen.'

'Shush!' she said, gently laying a finger across his lips.

The front door slammed shut with a bang. 'Missed it!' Hannah called, as she came hurtling into the room. 'Missed the school bus. What am I . . . What's all this?' she demanded, her expression of incredulity giving way to a beaming smile.

Jenny giggled and tore herself away from Tom. 'Hannah, let me set you straight. I'm not leaving Cragley. This is where I want to be.'

'I thought . . .'

'And I have no intention of marrying Will Renfrew. In fact, your dad and I . . .' She broke off to glance at Tom.

He nodded. 'It's true,' he said.

Hannah let out a whoop and raced out of the room, 'James!' they heard her calling up the stairs. 'James! Guess what.'

'We've started something now,' Tom said happily.

Jenny smiled and nodded. 'Haven't we just.'

The twins came into the room, faces flushed with excitement. 'I've told him!' Hannah said. 'I've told him you're staying and everything!'

'We're very pleased,' James confirmed. He

tried to be solemn, serious, but his face soon dissolved into a smile as big as Hannah's. Jenny got up to hug and kiss them both.

*　　*　　*

'Show her, Dad,' James said later.

'What?'

'You know!' Hannah insisted. She got up and brought across a couple of little stools from the far side of the kitchen. Jenny had already noticed them, and had admired them.

'Crackets,' Hannah said.

'We know the shop trade is a bit slack,' Tom said. 'So we put our heads together while you were away, to see if we could come up with anything to help.'

'You made these?' Jenny asked.

He nodded. 'They're called crackets. Just simple little things the pitmen used to make for themselves. Hannah noticed some in a pine shop in Morpeth.'

'They sell well, the woman there said,' Hannah added. 'She told me people like them as souvenirs, and for little children.'

'They are attractive,' Jenny said thoughtfully, turning one over in her hands.

'I thought I could make a few for you. And maybe one or two other small items of hand-crafted furniture? An extra line for the shop?'

'What a lovely idea! Thank you, Tom.'

'James, here, had an even better idea.'

153

James shrugged diffidently. 'On-line selling,' he said. 'Internet sales. You don't even need people coming to the shop.'

'I had wondered about that,' Jenny admitted. 'But you need a website, and . . .'

'A website, yes,' James said. 'I've designed one for you. It's just rough at the moment, but it could soon be made operational.'

'You've designed one!' Jenny shook her head. 'James, that's amazing.'

'We thought it might help.'

Jenny looked at the three of them, each in turn. 'Pool our resources?' she said, smiling. 'Is that what you were thinking? A family business?'

There were murmurs of agreement.

'What wonderful people you are!'

Tom looked relieved. 'Go and see what's happening in the outside world,' he told the twins.

'Your dad and I have a few things to discuss,' Jenny added. 'Quite a lot, actually.'

James and Hannah laughed and departed readily.

'What a wonderful morning!' Jenny smiled lovingly at Tom.

'What a wonderful life,' he murmured in return. 'Oh yes,' she agreed.

'Oh yes, indeed!'